"Let me go, Rush. Let me go back to France and save Gwen and Jackson."

He crossed the office to sit beside her once more. "I have friends all over the world, Lucy. We can track down where he's holding your sister and the baby. Let me make some calls."

"No! You can't alert anyone or he'll kill them. He gave me a week and it's going by too fast. The man following me might already suspect I caved and told you. It has to be his way."

"We'll find a better option," he promised.

She shook her head, tears blurring her vision again. "I'm not taking you down with me. Destroy the ghost files," she pleaded. "Wipe out all records of Garmeaux. Forget I was here."

"I can't do that." His voice turned hard again. "I won't do that."

She opened her mouth to say more and he smothered the words with a kiss. What might have originated as a kiss of comfort ignited like a match struck, blazing across her senses.

INVESTIGATING CHRISTMAS

USA TODAY Bestselling Authors

DEBRA WEBB & REGAN BLACK

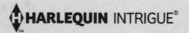

HARLEQUIN INTRIGUE®

For Debra, the best mentor, writing partner and friend in the
world! It's a joy to be on this marvelous adventure with you!

Recycling programs
for this product may
not exist in your area.

ISBN-13: 978-0-373-69945-2

Investigating Christmas

Printed in U.S.A.

www.Harlequin.com

Debra Webb, born in Alabama, wrote her first story at age nine and her first romance at thirteen. It wasn't until after she spent three years working for the military behind the Iron Curtain—and a five-year stint with NASA—that she realized her true calling. Since then the *USA TODAY* bestselling author has penned more than one hundred novels, including her internationally bestselling Colby Agency series.

Regan Black, a *USA TODAY* bestselling author, writes award-winning, action-packed novels featuring kick-butt heroines and the sexy heroes who fall in love with them. Raised in the Midwest and California, she and her family, along with their adopted greyhound, two arrogant cats and a quirky finch, reside in the South Carolina Lowcountry, where the rich blend of legend, romance and history fuels her imagination.

Books by Debra Webb and Regan Black

Harlequin Intrigue

Colby Agency: Family Secrets

Gunning for the Groom
Heavy Artillery Husband
Investigating Christmas

The Specialists: Heroes Next Door

The Hunk Next Door
Heart of a Hero
To Honor and To Protect
Her Undercover Defender

Visit the Author Profile page at Harlequin.com for more titles.

CAST OF CHARACTERS

Lucille Gaines—Lucy has recently moved to France for a new job as a personal assistant to a wealthy recluse. After a difficult year, she's bringing her sister and nephew along to give them all the fresh start they need.

Rush Grayson—Rush pulled himself out of a bleak childhood and a stint in juvenile detention for hacking into secure sites to create and position his company, Gray Box, at the top of the information-security industry.

Dieter Kathrein—The elderly billionaire lives a reclusive life in France. With Lucy as his new assistant living and working on one of his estates, he hopes to maintain his privacy amid a formidable electronic age.

Mathieu Garmeaux—A reporter based in Paris who has turned up what could be the story of his career.

Sam Bellemere—Rush's business and development partner, he serves as head of security for Gray Box, keeping an eye out for any attempts to break their system.

Chapter One

France, North of Paris
Tuesday, December 15, 5:40 p.m.

Lucy Gaines swapped her heels for flats for the short walk home from her new job. Her employer's butler watched patiently, opening the door when her heels were tucked into her tote.

"Have a lovely evening, Miss Gaines," he said in precise, formal French.

"Merci," she replied, crossing the threshold. Outside, she paused on the top step and breathed in the crisp evening air as the butler closed the magnificent oak door with a near-silent *whoosh*. Every day she marveled that she worked here, lived *here*.

December in France. It seemed her new reality might never sink in completely. Just over a month ago she'd been staring down the dark emotional tunnel of a melancholy holiday season in Chicago. Her life had once more taken a U-turn and this time she couldn't be happier. Practically skipping down the steps, she tugged at the collar of her wool coat, keeping the dropping temperature at bay although the brisk winter air here was balmy compared to the bite of the Windy City this time of year.

She lived and worked in a dream world. Chantilly and Paris were only a short drive away from this sleepy, rural neighborhood that barely qualified as a town. *Commune*, she corrected herself with the French term. Growing up, she and her sister, Gwen, had dreamed of trekking through Europe after college, immersing themselves in history, culture and new discoveries with each day. They'd made it, though the timing and circuitous route of ups and downs had been grueling for both of them.

Technically, Lucy's MBA from Stanford University made her overqualified for a position as a personal assistant. But Dieter Kathrein was no ordinary entrepreneur. A French billionaire known for his business acumen and reluctance to socialize, he'd promised her an experience and connections that would make even the interview worth her time.

Odd how she'd thought he was overselling it then, only to discover he'd left several perks off the original attractive list. Being able to walk to and from work was merely the start. Mr. Kathrein had shown an unexpected degree of generosity when he added a car and driver along with a rent-free cottage to her benefits package. With those worrisome personal details handled, the scales had tipped in favor of her accepting the position.

Obviously pleased to have her on board, his sharp gaze had turned misty under his bushy white eyebrows as he shared his family's rich history in this pocket of France. Lucy had been sucked in immediately, thoroughly captivated by the sad and brave story of Dieter's parents, killed while assisting the French Resistance against the Nazis. The sole survivor, barely out of his teens, he'd pledged his life to preserving the family legacy and ensuring the security of future Kathrein generations.

He's certainly done that, Lucy thought, soaking up the views and serene environment. Day in and day out, everything she could see belonged to the Kathrein estate. He and his wife must have been delighted to raise their two daughters in such an idyllic area—the perfect balance between the past and present, vibrant cities and quiet countrysides, staggering history and a lovely, hope-filled future.

She marveled that the man whose extreme preference for privacy and solitude had so graciously shared a corner of this sublime region with her and her remaining family. At the time he'd said, in his cultured French accent, "Family is the only reason to do anything in this world." She couldn't agree with him more.

Following her interview, once she'd signed the contracts, Dieter had entrusted her to the estate manager, who'd given her a full tour, culminating with a walk-through of the cottage. Considering the regal elegance of Dieter's sprawling residence she shouldn't have been so stunned by his definition of *cottage*. The four-bedroom manor house had two parlors, a dining room, a renovated kitchen and a sunroom downstairs—all fully furnished. The modern updates throughout the house had been expertly crafted to blend seamlessly with the original, old-world charm. She'd fallen in love with the space immediately, knowing this would be the fresh start she needed.

When she rounded the bend of the lane, the front door of the house came into view and Lucy's shoulders relaxed as the last of the day's challenges fell away. At ninety-six, and firmly set in his ways, her elderly boss could be more than a little difficult at times. Those speed bumps would smooth out in the weeks ahead. This wasn't her first experience with an eccentric boss who expected people and details to fall into place. For her part, she knew it was simply a matter of acclimating to his personality, communication style and priorities. The holiday season, with the influx of family and happy traditions, would help them both bridge that gap.

For now, work was behind her and she'd be home

momentarily. *Home* in France! The lovely thought brought a smile to her lips. In a minute or two, she'd be able to see the progress Gwen had made with the Christmas tree today and then she'd tickle a smile out of her nephew, Jackson. Only eight months old and already the little guy was an incurable flirt. On a second wind infused with happiness, she picked up the pace and hurried along the lane.

This wasn't how she'd pictured her life would be at twenty-six, but she thought the three of them were settling into a pleasant and hopeful routine as a family. Despite the headache of the overseas move—no one hated flying more than Lucy—Gwen seemed to smile more often, the grief fading from her eyes with each new day. Lucy celebrated every small, positive change in Gwen after the heartbreaking and unexpected loss of her husband only two months after Jackson's arrival in the world.

Having her sister and nephew around gave Lucy a much-needed anchor as she learned her new job and let go of her own heartbreak. Her loss had been mild in light of Gwen's tragedy, but moving from California to France, embracing a new career and direction in life, had helped them both.

"I'm home," Lucy called out as she walked through the front door. She set down her briefcase and purse to shrug out of her coat, hanging it on the antique hall tree. The house was quiet and she didn't hear any of the typical noises or catch any savory aromas from the kitchen. Maybe Gwen and Jackson were playing in the garden out back.

Lucy dropped off her purse and briefcase in the smaller parlor room at the front of the house they'd repurposed as her home office.

Kathrein had requested she keep flexible hours regardless of where she chose to live, since he had an unpredictable sleep pattern. Lucy had yet to seek out a social life, so it didn't bother her to be available whenever her boss woke with a concern or fresh idea.

"Where's my favorite little man?" Lucy sing-songed as she walked down the dim hallway. Her shoe caught in something and she bent for a closer look. One of Jackson's cotton blankets, she noticed, picking it up. How strange. Gwen, older by four years, had always been a bit compulsive about keeping things neat and tidy.

Lucy slid back the pocket door and stepped into the larger parlor they used as a family room. Her mind went blank. She couldn't make any sense of what she was seeing.

It looked as if a tornado had ripped right through the room, overturning furniture and twisting every-thing in its path. The fresh Christmas tree Dieter had had delivered to the house just days before was top-pled over. The pine scent rising from broken branches and crushed green needles weighted the air in the

room, making her queasy. The antique glass ornaments they'd inherited from their grandmother were
scattered and crushed, strewn along the floor like
sparkling, hazardous confetti.

No. *No.* The word echoed through Lucy's mind.
This disaster didn't make any sense. Gwen would
never make this kind of mess or leave it for someone
else to find. *Where are they?* Lucy's heart stalled
out in her chest.

"Gwen." What she'd intended as a shout came out
as a rasp. She cleared the terror from her throat and
tried again. "Gwen!" She raced to the kitchen. The
destruction wasn't as bad here, though the chairs were
out of place and Jackson's stroller was missing.

Maybe they'd missed the terror. Gwen often took
Jackson out for a walk before dinner. Lucy clung to
that hope right up until she noticed the cracked wood
frame around the back door latch. Fumbling with her
phone, she dialed Gwen's cell phone number. No answer. She ended the call before the voice mail greeting finished. Tears threatened to spill over as Lucy
raced upstairs, hoping the baby would be in his crib,
safe and oblivious to the destruction downstairs. Jackson wasn't there.

Her legs weak and shaking, she returned to the
kitchen and leaned against the countertop, struggling
to breathe. The signs were all too clear. Something
awful had happened to her sister and nephew. She

couldn't make her heart accept it. Picking her way through the house again, she searched for a note, missing valuables, anything to put this chaos into context.

She stood there, helpless and scolding herself. Calling 911 wouldn't help, and she didn't know the local equivalent to reach the police.

Who could possibly gain from targeting a widow and infant? Lucy didn't have enemies and very few friends were aware of her overseas move. She and Gwen had decided to save the announcement for the annual Christmas letter, a cheerful high point to counter the sadness of the past year. She dialed Gwen's number again and left a pitiful voice message this time, pleading for a reply.

Devastated, Lucy fell to her knees, the baby blanket she'd found in the hallway clutched to her chest. Her sobs tangled with fear and desperation. Who would do this? Crime in this area was practically nonexistent. Everyone they'd met in this quiet, isolated part of France had been friendly.

Too isolated to be random, a small voice in her head declared. Dieter Kathrein might be a recluse, but he was also a legend. The estate was well-known and he had enough staff to make it obvious when he was in residence. At his age, with his massive business success, he'd racked up a few enemies along the way. The attack could be retaliatory and Gwen and Jackson were taken by mistake.

Her boss could help. He would know who to call and he had nearly limitless resources. He'd help her navigate the system, help her through the next steps. His money and influence would make recovering Gwen and Jackson a priority for the authorities. On a surge of hope, Lucy went into her office, where she wouldn't have to look at the wreckage while she spoke with him.

She jumped a little when her cell phone rang in her hand. Gwen's number showed on the screen and Lucy's body sagged with relief. "Gwen! Where are you? Are you okay?"

"Lucy, we aren't hurt but you need to listen very carefully."

Gwen's voice, normally calm and strong, trembled with fear. The sound dragged Lucy back to that terrible day when her sister had called to say her husband had died. Gwen's sorrowful tears and inconsolable shock on that day still haunted Lucy. "Where are you?" she asked again.

"In—" Her sister's reply ended on a startled gasp.

"Lucille." Dieter Kathrein's curt tone confused and startled her all over again. "This call shall suffice as proof of life."

"Mr. Kathrein?" She'd left his offices less than an hour ago. Had the kidnappers grabbed Gwen and the baby and then attacked his house, as well? Whoever planned this knew how to cull the weak, seizing the elderly, a young mother and a helpless baby. "Are you injured?"

"I am well." He didn't sound the least bit rattled by the circumstances. In fact, this was the tone he used in his business conversations. "We are negotiating new terms."

"Pardon me, sir?"

His English was flawless, though gently rounded by a French accent when he was stressed or tired. Then the accent grew heavier and something else seeped in, drenching the words with a harsh elegance that was tougher to understand.

"Negotiating." He enunciated each syllable and added something at the end that sounded closer to German, which only confounded Lucy. "Your sister and her son are with me. They are safe. They will remain safe as long as you do as I say, young lady."

"You have Gwen and Jackson?" She squeezed her eyes shut and tried to wrap her mind around it but couldn't. Behind her closed eyelids she saw the mangled parlor, the broken bits of the few treasures they'd brought to France. "Why?" *How*, *when* and *where* all needed answering, as well, but she limited herself to one question at a time.

"They are leverage to ensure your cooperation,"

he stated, as if it should have been obvious. "You love your family, correct?"

"More than anything," she whispered. He knew how much those two people meant to her. Gwen and Jackson were all she had left. She and Gwen had lost their parents in a plane crash during Lucy's second year of undergrad. Gwen had been the steady, reassuring voice of reason when grief would have derailed Lucy's goals. She swore. "How could you do this?"

"As I thought. Look in your desk drawer. The top one. There is an envelope."

Thoroughly devastated, she did as he directed, withdrawing a plain white envelope. Only the weight of the paper gave away the means and quality of the man behind this treacherous attack.

"Did you find it?" he demanded.

"Yes," she replied, lowering her voice. Countering belligerence with a calm and composed response was a trick she'd learned in her MBA program. In her early days with Kathrein it had been surprisingly effective at defusing him when he grew agitated over something.

"Everything you need is in the envelope. A man seeking to ruin my grandson's political plans went digging through *my* background. My past is irrelevant! Nosy reporters," Kathrein ranted. "It is no more than slanted, ancient history and vicious rumors. My

Daniel is a good boy. He will *not* pay for the mistakes of my youth. Family is everything, yes?"

"Yes," she agreed. Apparently one member of his family—his only grandson and heir—was worth her entire remaining family combined. The envelope crinkled as her hands fisted, wishing she could wring his leathery, wrinkled neck. Her pulse hammered behind her temples. She had to think, to find a way around this. What kind of threat, what ancient secrets from his past had pushed the wealthy recluse to these drastic measures?

"The man stored electronic copies of these damaging rumors in a Gray Box," Kathrein said.

Gray Box. Memories that Lucy would rather have continued to forget emerged, vying for precedence in her troubled thoughts.

"As outlined in your instructions," he went on, "you will retrieve every document and then destroy everything in the cloud, removing all traces of the electronic records."

Break into a secure Gray Box? Kathrein had no idea what he was asking. Rush Grayson, the brilliant creator of that particular secure cloud storage service, had contracts with the United States military and intelligence agencies. His proprietary Gray Box encryption was *that* reliable and impossible to hack. To date, there had never been a successful breach. "What you're asking is impossible, Mr. Kathrein."

"You'd best hope not, Lucille. Since the man I contracted was not successful with the password and such, I presume it will require a more feminine ingenuity," he suggested.

Her mind caught on his words and suddenly his determination to bring her to France, to give her anything and everything she needed to make the transition became clear. She was as much a pawn as her sister and nephew, caught in a life and death game of speed chess. Dieter Kathrein didn't need a personal assistant as much as he'd anticipated a need for her to pry open software. He'd selected Lucy based on *her* past.

Oh, dear God.

"If you contact the police or anyone else I will terminate your family," he said. "If you fail I will terminate your family."

Renewed fear tightened her chest. "Mr.—"

"You have one week."

Her heart stumbled. Seven days to break into a Gray Box? He might give her a year and she wouldn't be able to deliver. No matter what she'd learned during her time with the company founder, she didn't have any confidence she could accomplish the task in the next decade. "Sir, I'm begging you to reconsider."

"Begging does not an ounce of good. Results matter to me. You know this. Retrieve the information or you will never see your family alive again."

If someone on Kathrein's extensive staff had already tried and failed to crack the secure storage site, she couldn't possibly hope to succeed long distance. The inevitable scenarios played like a house of horrors tour in her mind. "Wait! Please, I need more than a week." Lucy floundered for a believable excuse. "I'll have to return to the States." For the first time in years, the plane trip would be the least of her challenges.

"One week, Lucille. Not a single hour more."

"Don't hurt them," she pleaded. Silence was the reply. He'd ended the call. She reflexively redialed Gwen's number. No answer. Tears rolled down her cheeks. How could he threaten Jackson? Just last week, he'd stooped over the stroller and smiled warmly at the baby during one of Gwen's walks around the estate. Kathrein must have lost his mind. Clearly a crazy man held the lives of her sister and nephew in his arthritic hand. *Damn it*. No matter what her insane boss believed, cracking a Gray Box was not possible.

She upended the envelope and poked through the contents. Along with a substantial amount of cash, presumably to assist with her travel expenses, Kathrein had provided detailed background on investigative journalist Mathieu Garmeaux. How had this one man gathered secrets damaging enough to push Kathrein to such an extreme and irrational response?

Kathrein probably assumed Lucy could magically derive the man's username and password from the background. Not likely. She dashed away her tears with the back of her hand, forcing herself to concentrate on solutions rather than the cold dread sinking into her bones. If Garmeaux would be reasonable, if she could convince him to help her, maybe she could avoid a pointless attack on a secure Gray Box and she could get her family back by morning.

Nothing lost by asking, she decided. She booted up her laptop and did a preliminary search for the man based on the background provided. First she'd send an email and follow that with a phone call. Or not. Her stomach sank at the first search result.

Mathieu Garmeaux, based in Paris, had died two weeks ago, the victim of a traffic accident just a few blocks from his apartment.

Dear God. Lucy dropped her head into her hands and flexed her fingertips hard into her scalp, tugging on her hair as the dates lined up in her mind. She'd been with Mr. Kathrein in Paris at the time. In light of the kidnapping it seemed far more likely that the journalist's motorcycle had lost the fight with a panel truck on purpose. If Kathrein had had Garmeaux killed, what wouldn't he do to gain control of the documents?

A shudder racked her shoulders as she brought up an airline website and booked the next available flight to San Francisco. Gwen and Jackson were counting on her and, like Mr. Kathrein, she would do anything to save her family. Oh, she hated having even that much in common with the wretched old man. Air travel and returning to Rush Grayson's territory were small costs compared to the priceless value of the people who mattered most to her.

Her ticket booked, she tried not to think of anything but the next step and failed miserably. Knowing she'd be facing the man who'd broken her heart last year had her agonizing over every item of clothing as she packed. Circumstances aside, deceiving Rush went against her nature. Though he'd hurt her, she'd never wanted to hurt him. Saving Gwen and Jackson meant damaging the Gray Box reputation, and that left a sour taste in her mouth.

"Can't be helped," she said aloud. Zipping her luggage closed, she called for the car and driver to take her to the airport. As the estate faded into the distance behind the car, Lucy's thoughts bounced from past to present and leapfrogged into the near and distant future.

Starting with a business introduction and a surprising mutual respect, she and Rush had developed a friendship that had become so much more. Chills raced along her skin at the memories she couldn't suppress. She'd been foolish enough to fall in love and he'd been smart enough to adhere to his personal boundaries.

Despite the knowledge that their business interests and efforts had served them both well, she didn't entertain any illusion that he'd be particularly happy to see her on a personal level. What Kathrein required of her would push the mutual professional respect across a bed of hot coals.

If by some miracle she succeeded in her task, her foolish heart's persistent, feathery hope to someday reconcile with Rush would be blown out of reach forever.

Chapter Two

Rush Grayson returned to his new company head-quarters in the Financial District absolutely frustrated. He'd walked out on the morning meeting after more than an hour of zero progress. Time was precious and he refused to waste it. If the prospective client didn't experience an attitude adjustment soon, they could find a different security solution for their data. It wouldn't be as effective as the system he'd designed, but that wasn't his problem.

He'd learned the hard way to walk away and let go. His desire to help others didn't mean they wanted his help. He had to remember Gray Box was no longer at the point where one contract would make or break the company.

He took the express elevator up to the executive office suite and the stress fell away when the doors parted and he entered his domain. His journey to the top hadn't always been pretty, but he'd made sure the gorgeous view he enjoyed now rewarded him every day.

"Good morning, Melva." He paused at the receptionist's desk to pick up his messages. With a little more life experience than Rush or any of the other executives on the floor, the woman had been a godsend, keeping them all grounded with the discreet, calm professionalism he wanted to project to clients and competitors alike.

"How was the meeting?" she asked, peering at him over her bold, red cheaters.

"I lost patience and walked out." He shrugged. "How has the day been treating you?"

"Glorious, thank you." She flicked a hand at the stunning, panoramic views of San Francisco beyond the glass walls surrounding the space. "Your messages." She slid a stack of small paper squares across the marble counter.

Rush grinned. Although everything within Gray Box systems was completely electronic now, she insisted on backing up phone message emails with her old-school habit. He loved it.

"You have a visitor waiting in your office." Melva's practiced smile turned warm, almost affectionate.

The expression stopped Rush short. Melva had used that particular soft smile with only one person and that person was now rusticating in France, working for a musty old man with almost as much money as Rush. He turned slowly toward his office suite, which occupied one full corner of the floor, noticing the brunette seated in the waiting area near his assistant's desk.

"Where is Trisha?"

Melva's lips flatlined with disapproval at the mention of his assistant's name. She'd never warmed to his current girlfriend. It didn't help that since he and Trisha had been involved personally, he had yet to find a more suitable place for her within the company. "It appears she is away from her desk," Melva stated.

His gaze swept over the other glass-walled offices and conference rooms. "I can see that." Just as he could see the long, glossy sweep of his unexpected guest's hair falling straight and sleek well past her shoulders. His pulse kicked, though he knew it couldn't be the woman he most wanted to see. Despite Melva's warmth, he knew that very special brunette was in France. Still, his body moved automatically, propelling him closer as if hope alone would change the stark reality.

He wanted to stride on into his office like a consummate professional, giving his assistant room to do her job and make introductions, but Trisha wasn't anywhere on the floor. He could go back downstairs and catch the private elevator that opened into the hallway behind his posh office. That would create an entrance worthy of the primary developer and top dog at Gray Box.

Or he could stop being ridiculous and get on with his day. Hadn't he been lamenting time wasters a few minutes ago? Irritated with himself, he strode forward to meet his guest.

The familiar vanilla-laced scent stopped him as effectively as a brick wall. His heart slammed against his ribs when she looked up and he saw those big brown eyes full of nerves.

"Lucy?" He had to be hallucinating. She'd left him a year ago, effectively disappearing overnight. One day here—and his—and the next, he been left holding a note that she'd moved to Chicago with no plans to return. He folded his arms over his chest, not giving a damn about defensive posture. She didn't look capable of rendering destruction, but he knew better. "This is..." The multiple ways to finish that sentence became a logjam in his head.

"A surprise, I'm sure," she finished for him, coming to her feet.

He had to back up a step to stay out of her personal space and to keep his hands to himself.

"My apologies for dropping in unannounced, Rush." Her smile flashed and disappeared from one second to the next. "I just got back in town. Can you spare a few minutes?"

Hearing her say his name brought back images and memories best left until later. "For you, always." He caught the subtle twist of her lips and winced. His time and attention had been the one sore spot during their relationship. They were both busy professionals and he couldn't always insist that global markets and prestigious clients wait while he wrapped up a date.

Things were different now, calmer and more predictable since he'd achieved his goal and positioned his company at the forefront of the electronic information security industry. *Calmer, but not nearly done*, he thought, as part of his brain slid back to the wasted morning meeting.

Recognizing the doubt about his availability in Lucy's eyes, he pulled his attention back to the present. Bending over Trisha's keyboard, he sent his secretary a text alert to clear his calendar for the afternoon. "There." He stood tall, smiling at Lucy. "I'm all yours for the rest of the day." The idea of it cascaded over him in a wave of effervescent anticipation. Only Lucy had ever had this effect on him. He held open his office door, encouraging her to enter ahead of him. The soft fabric of the smart evergreen dress she wore swirled at her knees, and he enjoyed the distraction for a moment.

When the door closed behind him, he flipped the switch that turned the clear glass panes of his office opaque, giving them privacy from anyone else on the floor. "What do you need?"

"Oh, my," she breathed. "Your view of the bay is stunning." Lucy turned a slow circle in the middle of his office, a bittersweet smile wobbling on her lips as she took it all in. "The world at your feet, right?"

"I saved the best view for myself," he confessed.

"As you should." Her smile blossomed, a little less wistful. She cleared her throat. "The building, the new offices…it's all amazing, Rush. Congratulations. You deserve it."

"You think so?" Pride swelled up at her praise before he could battle it back. He'd never reconciled the way she'd constantly encouraged him with the fact that she'd walked away without a single word of warning. Never one to leap without looking, her sudden departure from him as well as the city had completely baffled him.

She nodded, interlocking her fingers at her waist. He remembered that little habit showing up whenever her self-control was about to snap. What was going on?

He shrugged out of his sport coat and hooked it on a sleek stainless coat tree near the door. "Why don't we sit down," he suggested briskly. He considered rounding his desk, emphasizing his position and power in the room. Instead, he moved toward the long, elegant leather couch. How many days had he envisioned her right here beside him with a cup of coffee in the morning or a glass of wine after a long day?

Lucy chose a chair on the other side of the art deco glass coffee table and that spark of hope that this might be a personal visit withered.

He catalogued every nuance and change as she settled into the chair. Fit as ever, her sense of style still radiated elegance and class. Yes, her hair had grown longer over the past year. And the warmth in her big brown eyes was tempered with something he couldn't pinpoint. She'd done her eyes with subtle color, framed by those thick, dark lashes, and she'd swept soft gloss over her rosy lips. He didn't care for the tense lines bracketing her lovely mouth. What had happened to her since she'd left him?

He'd kept tabs on her, always in search of a way to bring her back home to California. Not finding the right combination of timing and opportunity, he'd been forced to admit defeat and move on. He hadn't managed to forget her, even after sinking all his energy into a year of aggressive corporate growth and dodging the grasping pursuit of equally aggressive, gold-digging women.

He waited, offered her coffee and water. She graciously refused, but didn't seem willing to explain what had brought her here. "I heard about your brother-in-law," he said, breaking the silence. "I'm sorry for your loss."

"Thank you," she replied, her gaze drifting past him to the view of the bay.

"How is Gwen holding up?"

"Better day by day." Lucy's big brown eyes shimmered with tears until she blinked them away. "I think." White teeth momentarily nipped at her full lower lip. "Moving to France helped all of us."

That caught him off guard. "I didn't realize she went with you."

Lucy nodded. "Her son, Jackson, is eight months old. It's amazing watching him grow."

The worry in her eyes launched an internal battle as his need to shield himself battled against his need to comfort her. "Strong name." As he'd hoped, the words brought out her smile. She'd often lamented her name was a hurdle in the corporate world.

God, he couldn't take his eyes off her, stunned and delighted to have her in his office. Terrified he'd drop his heart into her hands and she'd reject the gift again. His palms itched to touch her, to hold her fine-boned hand in his again. How many nights had he tossed and turned, wishing for one more touch of her lips, gentle as rose petals, against his skin? Her chest lifted on a deep inhale and sent his mind on a sensual, inappropriate detour.

"I know you're busy," she began, "so I'll be brief. I could use a job, Rush. If you can find a place for me."

He knew the perfect place for her, though it had nothing to do with the professional answer she was seeking. Sitting forward, he propped his elbows on his knees. She knew him too well to bother hiding his excitement about bringing her on board. "A job here, with me?"

"With Gray Box." Her lips pursed. "France has been a great experience. Beyond beautiful, but—"

"We have plenty of wine country here," he interrupted. A voice in his head roared at him to shut up. He was an idiot to think she reminisced over their weekend adventures the way he did. He'd heard how quickly she'd replaced him with a new man in Chicago.

Her lips curled into another distant smile and she smoothed her hands over her dress. "California is home," she finished.

"I'm glad to hear you've come to your senses," he teased.

Her serious brown gaze didn't share his humor. "Do you have any openings?"

He glanced past her, had to assume Trisha's desk remained empty on the other side of the privacy-frosted glass. "I could use a personal assistant," he said, making the decision as he spoke.

"You're well aware I have an MBA. Maybe I can be of more use in—"

"Your current post is what, precisely?" Her gaze turned sharp with a hint of temper and he knew he had her just where he wanted her. Well, professionally anyway.

"Yes, my current title is personal assistant," she allowed. She crossed her legs at the ankle, distracting him again with far more intimate memories. "When I took the post with Dieter Kathrein everyone involved knew I was overqualified."

"I can assure you as *my* personal assistant you'll have more challenges."

"I'm sure you're right." Lucy tilted her head toward the desk on the other side of his office. "What about your current assistant?"

"She's not the dedicated PA I need," he countered. "Trisha manages my calendar and answers the phone right now, but it's a stopgap measure. She doesn't have your business acumen and I don't have time for her to develop it." The ease of his admission didn't surprise him. He'd always been able to talk with Lucy about anything.

Her dark eyebrows arched and her lips parted for a moment, then she clamped her mouth shut. "I see. Tell me more."

"We've been searching for a better fit for her

within the company," he added. "What were your duties with Kathrein?"

She shook her head, her gaze dropping to her hands. "Beyond telling you I managed his calendar, the rest of my responsibilities are confidential."

"Right. Of course." He waved that off as unimportant and quickly outlined his professional expectations. A savvy, analytical mind like Lucy's could help him keep Gray Box at the top and develop new ideas and market applications. She would be the perfect liaison between him and clients who waffled around wasting his time, too. "What do you think?"

"Salary and benefits?"

"Name it, whatever you need. I'll make sure it's all written into the contract." He twisted, pointed out a building across the street. "You can even have the corporate suite at the hotel until you find a place to live."

"That's very generous. Thank you." Her smile didn't quite reach her eyes as she accepted the ridiculous offer.

"You're worried about *me*, aren't you?" He sat back, stretched his arms across the back of the couch. "About our history?"

"No," she said, her denial a little weak. "I came to you as a colleague and friend. We both have new interests, now. You can reassure Trisha or whomever you're seeing that I won't interfere with your personal life."

He didn't appreciate that promise or the vague reprimand. Lucy had been his only "interest" for over a year. She still was, if he was brutally honest about it. The women who'd followed her had floated through his life without any real substance or impact. Contrary to rumors, he didn't date in the traditional sense of connecting to someone. Trisha was the latest in a line of women willing to spend time as his public companion in exchange for his opening a few professional doors for her.

"I won't lie, Lucy. I've missed you. If you want to reconnect personally, I'm all for it."

Her eyes went wide. "Rush."

He flared his hands, let them fall. "Call it full disclosure. When it comes to you and me, the ball is in your court. If you're here for purely professional reasons, I respect that."

"I am." She swallowed. "Thank you for the job. You won't regret it."

He already did. Lucy Gaines had been everything he'd wanted from a woman in both his personal and professional worlds. Smart and kind, lovely and compassionate, they'd shared interests from wine country to stock market trends to pitching in with local charities.

"Let's get out of here." If they stayed in this office,

he'd be tempted to unload every stray business idea he'd wanted to discuss with her over the past year. Not only would that border on employee abuse, it would leave him wide open and vulnerable. He wanted her, he intended to have her, but only when he knew she'd stick around. Standing, he urged her to her feet as well. "I'll show you what's changed since you left." Reflexively he checked his watch.

"Only everything," she said with a short laugh. "Don't wreck your entire day for me. I'm sure Melva can fill me in and give me instructions about the hotel suite."

He picked up on the edge creeping into her voice. How could he convince her he wanted to give her every minute today? "Melva is absolutely capable," he agreed. "We can skip the full tour if you're tired from the trip." He wasn't sure why he was pressing her, only that he wasn't ready to let her out of his sight. She was everything he remembered and more, but he got the feeling she was hiding something about her time with Kathrein. He didn't stand a chance of figuring it out if he left her alone.

"I feel fine, Rush," she said, her smile tight. "We've agreed to terms. You don't have to entertain me."

"Ouch." He laid a hand over his heart, feigning pain. "I'm going to play tour guide anyway. There's no one better than me to bring you back up to speed, on Gray Box specifically and the Bay Area in general."

She shook her head, but not before he noticed the little lift at the corner of her mouth. His arrogance had often amused her. He switched off the privacy glass and caught sight of Trisha at Melva's reception desk. An even better reason to leave the office behind for the afternoon, he decided. While he'd been honest about searching for a better post for Trisha, he hadn't focused on the issue. Now he had an excellent reason to move forward on that adjustment immediately.

"You know," he said, turning his back on the rest of the executive floor, "I should start the tour right here." He gestured toward the door in the opposite wall, tucked behind a floor-to-ceiling display case filled with books and myriad industry awards. "My indispensable PA should know my secret escape route." He led her out of the office and into a narrow service hallway. "Private bathroom," he said, pointing out another door. "There's a bedroom as well."

"A *bedroom*? Good grief, Rush. It's a wonder you haven't been sued for harassment."

Well, that stung. The gossip rags and paparazzi greatly exaggerated his personal exploits whenever he chose to spend time around town with models or actresses. "It's not a space I share," he replied through clenched teeth. When and why had her opinion of him plummeted so drastically? "You know how things go during research or a product launch, or—"

"When you're closing a major deal," she finished for him. "I remember."

He swallowed the urge to point out if he wasn't constantly focused on building up the business, Gray Box wouldn't be such a convenient fallback option for her. Except a woman with Lucy's skills and credentials could name her salary and benefits, and choose from numerous offers. Knowing that, knowing how talented she was, it was tough to accept she'd returned to him without any intent to rekindle their personal relationship. He couldn't decide if his decision to hire her made him an easy mark, sentimental or selfish. Time would tell.

"This is my private elevator." He reached out and punched the button. "Most of the time I use the public one or the express, but occasionally this is necessary."

One side of her mouth curled in a half smile. "You pulled out all the stops here," she said.

If she'd seen his heart on his sleeve as he eagerly shared this with her, she didn't give him any reaction. "The office isn't just about the show of power, though it helps." The doors parted and he ushered her inside. Her fragrance, the dark sensual notes smoothed with a whisper of vanilla, filled the small space. He hoped the scent lingered a while so he could breathe her in at will. He punched the button for three floors down, pulling himself together. That spark they'd once shared seemed to be missing now and it wasn't her problem that he hadn't been able to get over her.

"This must make it easier to avoid distractions," she murmured.

"Exactly." So she remembered how people cornered him in elevators, pitching ideas and résumés.

"As your PA, is it my job to fend them off now?" Her gaze narrowed and she pretended to glare at potential intruders lurking in the corners.

"No." He laughed a little and then reconsidered. Though she stood several inches shorter, even in the heels, she could be formidable. "Well, maybe."

The doors parted and he escorted her to the human resources department. After making introductions, the department manager sat down with both of them, drawing up the details they'd agreed upon for Lucy's employment. Once the legalities were out of the way, Rush insisted on taking her down to the waterfront for a late lunch.

"You don't have to convince me to stay," she repeated when they were seated at a table with a stunning view. "I've signed the contract."

"This is my new favorite place," he said. He'd wanted to bring her here since it opened. "The food is better than the view."

She tilted her head, clearly surprised by his gushing endorsement. When her gaze followed his to the bay, he heard her sigh a little. "I didn't expect to miss it so much."

He was determined to bridge the gap, to earn the trust of the one woman he'd always been able to confide in. "What really brings you back here?"

Her eyes went wide and her chin dropped a little. "I was homesick."

He wasn't accepting that anymore. "A year ago it appeared Chicago was home," he countered. He paused while they gave the waitress their drink order. "Then you moved the family to France." What had happened over there?

She studied him a long moment. "Are you having second thoughts already?"

"No way." He shrugged. "I'm the luckiest CEO in the city. You could write your own ticket anywhere." In the back of his mind, he couldn't make it all add up. Better just to ask. "I'd like to know why me and why now?" He couldn't shake the feeling that she needed him to leap out in front of her and fight off an invisible enemy.

He'd be an idiot if he hadn't already considered and discarded the idea of corporate espionage. Lucy didn't play unethical games. While following her career meant he had a basic knowledge of Kathrein's business interests, the older man hadn't shown any intention of seriously competing with Gray Box.

"Kathrein didn't send me here to spy on you." Her

words proved how well they knew each other. "If he had made such a suggestion, I would have refused."

"I know." He recognized the steel in her gaze, respected it. He could take her "homesick" answer at face value or ruin lunch with an argument. Taking the high road, he turned the conversation to other topics. He would wait her out. They were too alike, had been too close, for her to keep any secrets from him for long.

The waitress came by with drinks and he ordered the lunch special for both of them, with Lucy's approval. "When we're done here, we can go on to the suite. It should be big enough for you and your family in the short term."

"Don't worry about that," she interjected. "Gwen and Jackson are staying in France through the holidays. That gives me time to find a place."

"Really?" That set off alarm bells. Unlike him, Lucy had been raised in a close-knit family. She and Gwen had only grown more inseparable when they lost their parents. "Will you go back to be with them over Christmas?"

"I'm not sure yet." She gazed out over the water, apparently captivated by the traffic on the bridge.

"Talk to me, Lucy." Something was way off. He reached across the table and covered her hand with his. "What happened in France?"

She closed her eyes and gave her head a quick

shake. "Nothing. Nothing," she repeated. Opening her eyes, she gave him a hard, forced smile. "Gwen and I decorated the most amazing Christmas tree last weekend. Her eye for design is remarkable, despite putting all the fragile ornaments near the top, out of Jackson's reach. He's crawling now, pulling himself up every chance he gets and he's very curious."

"So why wouldn't you go back for Christmas?"

"The flights," she said. "And I wasn't sure how things would go here, if I'd have the time off."

"We'll be closed the entire week." He paused as the waitress delivered two plates piled high with aromatic rice noodles, shrimp, and colorful shredded cabbage and vegetables. While they ate, he steered the conversation toward the charitable effort she'd insisted he dive into before she vacated his life. Using the wealth of brain power at Gray Box, he coordinated tutors for kids in need—those falling behind in school and those eager for a chance to leap ahead.

"Wow. You've made serious progress." This time her smile and eyes showed equal enthusiasm.

She could soak up the views until her homesickness faded while he enjoyed the even lovelier view of her. The deep, soulful eyes, those high cheekbones and that tender mouth were igniting fires in him that only she could tend. "We'll launch a new tech-focused camp next summer. I'll start scouting ideal sites soon." That would be the perfect assignment for Trisha, he realized. She knew the city well, enjoyed being out and being seen, and it would keep her away from the executive floor. Pleased with himself, he apologized to Lucy and sent quick text messages to Trisha and his HR department.

"Forgive me," he said, catching the small frown on Lucy's face. "I just thought of something that would move the process along."

She waved it away. "Don't worry about it."

"Appreciate that." He tucked his phone back into his pocket. Good grief, he'd missed her low-maintenance acceptance of his nature balanced by her high-energy ambition to reach her goals. Why had she walked out on the amazing chemistry they'd shared?

The question was right there on the tip of his tongue and he had to bite it back repeatedly as they left the restaurant for a walk through the marketplace and then on to explore a few other nearby changes in the city. He kept his hands in his pockets, away from her, reminding himself today they were two old friends catching up. Having cleared his calendar for the afternoon, he wanted to make the most of this precious time with her.

She'd helped him push harder toward his goals even as she wrapped up her graduate work. The day she'd presented her thesis, he'd been in the back row of the auditorium, silently cheering her on to victory.

They'd celebrated that night and memories of getting creative with the second bottle of champagne in the bedroom still powered his fantasies a year later.

He'd missed her so damn much. Not just the sex, though that had been amazing, but simple conversations, her quiet appreciation of the small things people overlooked as they pushed to get ahead. Lucy had a gift for seeing through the puzzling motivations of people behind the deal and it still annoyed him that he'd taken that gift—among her other talents—for granted.

Regardless of her true reasons for coming home, Rush vowed that this time around he wouldn't let her slip through his fingers.

Chapter Three

As the cable car moved west up California Street, Lucy wished she could escape to her hotel room and hide until morning. She needed time and space to boost her resolve. More, she needed some distance from Rush's warm conversation and familiar gestures and habits before she dumped all her problems into his capable hands. Kathrein's terrible threats, echoing incessantly in her head, kept her silent.

"You okay?" Rush nudged her shoulder. "We can hop off and take a taxi if that's better."

"This is wonderful." The boyish grin on his face was as infectious as it was charming and she grinned back. "San Francisco has such a different scent and pace than rural France."

"Rural?"

"I worked with Kathrein primarily on his estate near Chantilly. Only a few streets made up the nearest town." She didn't trust herself to mention the brief trip to the Paris office. "It surprised me how quickly the cities faded into serene countryside."

"Same thing happens here."

She swallowed the lump in her throat as his words stirred up lovely memories. The two of them had enjoyed great weekend drives north into wine country and south to hike and sail around the coastline. Though they'd tossed around the idea of traveling abroad, her reluctance to fly and his busy schedule limited their recreational choices. "I suppose you're right."

As they came into the heart of Nob Hill, pretty as a postcard on this clear afternoon, she admired the surrounding architecture and the latest restoration efforts Rush pointed out.

Her heart lurched in her chest, knowing his efforts this afternoon would be the last of their friendly moments. When he learned the truth, he'd be so furious with her and himself that even a professional reconciliation would be impossible. It was highly possible he'd destroy her career.

He'd been too eager to bring her on at Gray Box, letting her dictate all the terms. Eventually he'd demand real answers about why she'd walked away and she appreciated his candor about leaving any potential revival of their personal life up to her. He'd never cleared his calendar for her before and this time—

when it should've been the sweetest of gestures—she was using him.

Her ruse, although necessary, made his generous compliments about her skills ring hollow. She hated deceiving him and soon he would hate her for duping him. During the long flights, she'd come to the conclusion that she would never be able to fulfill Kathrein's demands and save her family without getting caught. This wasn't some average company she was trying to infiltrate. This was Rush's design. The man had successfully hacked into sensitive government sites as a middle schooler. With every ongoing minute she despised herself more for this charade. Finding a chink in the Gray Box armor was the only way to save her sister and nephew, and Rush didn't deserve the inevitable fallout of what she had to do.

Rock and a hard place, she thought. There were no good options. Even with more time, she had no chance of finding where Kathrein had hidden Gwen and Jackson on her own. The Kathrein real estate holdings offered the old man too many options on top of his endless resources.

As the cable car neared the last stop on the line, a motorcycle passed by, raising the hair at the back of her neck in a little shiver of fear as she thought of the reporter's accident in Paris. Kathrein had shown her only the wise, occasionally cranky old gentleman when she'd interviewed and subsequently worked for him, effectively masking his ruthless streak.

Rush politely offered his hand as they hopped off the cable car at the stop. "Why don't we head up to the Presidio?"

"We're not tourists," she replied. "And it's a long walk in these shoes."

His gaze slid down over her legs, and her body warmed as if he'd touched her. "I can fix that." He pulled out his phone and started texting.

She suppressed the urge to roll her eyes at him. Of course the hunky billionaire could fix a long walk. Rush loved cars. Just before her move to Chicago, he'd been debating about whether he should invest in an existing car service or purchase a dedicated fleet.

"The driver will meet us on Polk," Rush said, turning down the block. "Did you rent a car?"

It took her a moment to process such a normal question. "No. It was more practical to catch a shuttle from the airport and book a hotel within walking distance of your office."

"Practical and expensive." Rush frowned a little, the expression she remembered as intense concentration.

She knew better than to interrupt whatever puzzle his brilliant mind was sorting out. Her warm affection for him persisted, despite the time and distance. *My burden to bear*, she thought, with some desperation.

He might have said the ball was in her court, but re-kindling their relationship would make this all worse. She'd left him when she recognized she would never be his first priority. Walking away from him had been the hardest choice of her life up to that point. She'd never expected him to put her ahead of everything in his world—she'd only wanted to know she ranked among his general top five priorities. As much as she respected the building phase of his business, consistently settling for last place wasn't in her nature.

"You really don't have to spend the afternoon with me," she said as they glanced in store windows.

In the past, when they'd walked this route, he might have taken her hand or draped an arm around her shoulders. Today, they were two comfortable friends out in the city. She told herself to enjoy it while it lasted. By this time next week she wouldn't have even that much of him.

"I've missed you," he replied. "I don't want to be anywhere else."

Her heart skipped, wanting to imbue those words with significance and meaning. She reminded herself he missed discussing business or market shares or how to fine-tune client proposals with her. He might miss the sexual attraction, though she knew there was no shortage of women willing to take her place in his bed.

Any dent in her ego over that fact was her own

fault. She couldn't blame him for moving on after she'd walked away.

She searched for a neutral topic. "Why were you late to the office this morning?"

"Potential client. You might still be waiting in the office if I hadn't walked out."

"You didn't." She shook her head.

"Don't give me that look." He shrugged, eyeing a display in a florist's window. "They kept talking in circles. A complete waste of time." His eyebrows bobbed above his dark sunglasses. "You can smooth it all over for me tomorrow. That will be fantastic."

Her opinion of his assessment had to wait as the car arrived and Rush gave the driver their destination.

"So what did you decide about the car service?"

"You remember that?"

"Vaguely." She nodded. She'd thrown herself into work and freelancing, using her remaining energy for Gwen, and still her heart and mind had replayed every marvelous and frustrating minute she'd enjoyed with the man beside her. "So which was it?"

"Made the most sense to buy a small fleet and hire drivers for the day-to-day," he said.

She didn't ask about the weekends, knowing all too well how he'd enjoyed taking out his expensive cars for their road trips. On the short drive across town, she returned to the topic of his client, doing her best to remind them both she was his employee and they could conduct business regardless of the setting. He seemed determined to be contrary and leave business at the office today, pointing out new restaurants along with their old favorites.

When the car dropped them near the park, she resolutely turned her back on the yacht harbor and Rush's house on Marina Boulevard, where she'd spent far too much time with him during their last few months together.

They strolled along in a companionable silence and she savored the sunshine and crisp breezes blowing in from the bay. It was good to be home and this could very well be her last chance to enjoy the area. If she succeeded in rescuing her family, Rush would hardly allow her to walk away unscathed. Whether or not he understood her reasons, the only way to save his reputation would be to expose who caused the breach.

A strand of her hair caught in her lip gloss, and as she flipped her head she caught Rush staring at her. "Why are you looking at me that way?"

His lips quirked up at one corner and he raised a hand to her hair before he checked the motion. "You're lovely."

She focused on her breathing while he continued to study her.

"I changed my mind," he announced.

Her knees turned to jelly at those four words. He couldn't mean it. She needed to be on the inside of

Gray Box if she had any chance at all of recovering the journalist's documentation for Kathrein and saving her family. "About what?" She forced the question through her stiff lips while she moved to the nearest available bench.

"You should move into the house on Marina," he said, sitting down. "I know I offered the corporate suite, but you've always loved the bay views."

Her stomach bucked at the idea. She couldn't impose on his hospitality, couldn't possibly move in to the guest suite there while he was down the hall with a new girlfriend. The evenings they'd watched the sun set over the bay, glass of wine in hand, swept through her in a tide of nostalgic agony. Not to mention how impossible it would be to meet Kathrein's demands with Rush in the same house.

"That's hardly walking distance to the office." She presented the most logical argument first, praying he didn't counter with a suggestion to carpool. As he'd outlined her responsibilities, she would be with him much of the time, but not enough that they could get away with only one car. Public transit was decent in San Francisco, but she'd rather rely on her own two feet during the brief time she planned to be here.

"So choose a car. You know I have plenty. Or I can assign a driver to you."

Her mouth dropped open. "Rush, that's crazy," she said. The prickly conversation, so similar to being hired by Kathrein, made her queasy. What was it with billionaires tossing money around?

"Impulsive, maybe," he allowed. "Not crazy." He tapped a finger to the corner of his lips. "Whatever happened in France, the tension is showing on your face. I want to make this transition as easy as possible for you."

His astute observations weren't helping. "That's the stress of travel," she said. "You know how I am. You've done enough by giving me the job."

That unrepentant grin returned with a vengeance. "The job is one more excellent reason to stay in the boathouse," he said, using a drastically understated term for the coveted property.

"Not a good plan. I'd charge you overtime if you knocked on my bedroom door in the middle of the night with a scheduling conflict." Joking with him was her only way through this ridiculous quagmire.

"I can afford it," he assured her with a cocky grin.

"You say that now." She hadn't been fooled by his vague references to Trisha. As a way to prepare for the interview, she'd checked out recent social headlines about Rush. His current secretary-girlfriend would be furious that he'd extended the boathouse offer. She didn't want to wreak havoc in his personal life, too. Once she had what Kathrein needed, she would be gone. She couldn't let Rush burn through any bridges while she was here. "Does Trisha use one of your personal vehicles?"

"She doesn't drive," he replied with a one-shoulder shrug.

Leave it to Rush to miss the bigger point. He was insulting all three of them, and oblivious or not, she couldn't let him get away with it. "The hotel suite is the better choice for me right now."

"Too bad. It's booked. I just remembered."

She gave him a long look. "Really?"

He nodded and the lie was patently transparent in his eyes and his grin.

She had no business being amused by the man. She needed to treat him as her boss. "As your personal assistant, I can verify that easily enough, and I'll add it's no problem for me to stay where I am."

"Starting tomorrow you can verify whatever you want. Right now, as a friend, you'll have to take my word on it." He leaned back on the bench stretching his arms wide, much as he had in his office, providing an outstanding impersonation of a king regarding his domain.

She didn't mind. Humble wasn't his best look. Confidence should go hand in hand with being one of the wealthiest men in the world. The start-ups he'd sold in his twenties had netted him billions, and thanks to the dynamic software powering Gray Box, his net worth increased exponentially year after year.

"You didn't pull out the timing argument when we were talking business on the drive over here."

"I was being polite," he said. "Honoring your topic of choice and bringing you up to speed simultaneously."

"I'm not staying at the house on Marina." He needed to accept her choice though she knew he didn't approve of it. "Thanks for the offer."

"Consider it an order instead of an offer," he pressed, lowering his voice.

"Is that supposed to be a threat?" If so, he needed a few lessons from Kathrein.

He arched an eyebrow. "Any hotel is way too public if that scheduling conflict occurs to me in the middle of the night. Think of the rumors when I storm the castle. The company stock could plummet."

She rolled her eyes, grateful once more for the sunglasses. "You won't storm anything. I'm *not* moving in with you. That's demanding too much from a PA." Too late she realized how that sounded. They'd had a similar argument when they'd been dating. He'd wanted her to move in and she'd insisted on maintaining her own apartment, despite the amount of time she spent with him. If there was a way to make this awkward reunion worse, she'd found it.

His body had gone utterly still and the only movement was the breeze ruffling his thick black hair. She hadn't noticed until now that he was overdue for a trim. He probably thought she was here to win him back as much as to secure a high-paying job.

"I don't live there anymore," he said, his voice tight. "I bought a condo down on Fremont Street."

"Oh." She couldn't bring herself to ask when he'd moved out or if it was because of her. Those questions put too much emphasis on her, when Rush's choices and actions should be all about what was best for him and his business. It made her inexplicably sad.

"Closer to the office." He stood up suddenly, shoved his hands deep into his pockets. "Why don't we get you moved in right now?"

"Stop it. I'm not moving into one of your personal properties." A slightly hysterical laugh bubbled out of her. "As the proud owner of one suitcase, I think I can manage it when you relent and give me the corporate suite."

"One suitcase?" He frowned at her. "You moved back home with one suitcase?"

Her pulse skittered over that unwise slip. She scrambled for excuses. "You know I travel light," she reminded him. "And…and everything else is in storage," she fibbed. "Besides, I wasn't sure you'd give me the job."

He pushed his sunglasses up to his hair and his eyes were hard. "Have you forgotten everything about me? Everything about us?"

Unfortunately it seemed as if the specific details

of their relationship, both good and bad, would haunt her forever. Although she'd made sure he heard that she met someone else in Chicago, the rumor hadn't been true. The first white lie in what was turning into a lengthy list. Shame rolled through her and she averted her gaze to the magnificent rotunda and the curve of the colonnades behind him.

"Is there someone else?" Rush demanded. "Someone who would be upset or jealous if you accepted my hospitality?"

Resigned, she gave him as much honesty as possible. "Only Trisha," she replied.

"Let me worry about her."

"All right." She certainly didn't want to worry about the woman. "I don't want to cause any more friction than necessary taking this job." She wanted to gain access, recover the documents and hopefully get away before Rush realized what happened.

"And I'm telling you she won't be a problem."

"Okay." Lucy still couldn't look at him.

"Come on," he said abruptly. "Let's get your one suitcase moved into the boathouse." He held up a hand when she started to protest again. "Call it a new perk. The boathouse and job go together as of right now."

"You're being absurd. I'd rather you treated me like a normal employee."

"That's impossible and you know it," he argued. "When you talk your sister into visiting for the holidays, you'll appreciate my decision. Allow me to be considerate."

"Dictatorial is more accurate." She rubbed a hand over her heart, easing the ache at the mention of her family. Counting today, she had six more days to be sure Gwen and Jackson lived to see Christmas.

"Not even close." His lips—lips she'd loved kissing—flattened. "You can always turn the job down."

Oh, how she wished that was true, that her return to San Francisco was a simple case of homesickness. Being on the inside was her only real chance of breaking the Gray Box security within Kathrein's time frame. "Fine. If you say the boathouse goes with the job, so be it."

His mouth curled into a smug, satisfied smile. "Would you rather have a car or a driver at your disposal?"

"Neither." She laughed at the idea of having her own driver.

"It's my terms or no terms, Lucy."

Her heart skipped again at the familiar sound of her name on his lips. "You realize HR thinks all the terms are settled," she said.

"They answer to me." That dark eyebrow arched again, daring her to push him. Rush would happily flex his influence and get his way. He didn't hear the word *no* often enough and he wouldn't hear it from her, either. Not this time.

"I'll accept the generosity of the boathouse and the most efficient car available, on the condition that you'll allow me to move as soon as I'm reestablished here."

He nodded and stuck out his hand. "Deal."

"Thank you."

With another quick text, Rush had the car and driver waiting for them when they reached the south side of the park.

"I think you're more stubborn than ever." She sank into the supple leather upholstery of the backseat.

"Not a chance." He laughed. "I haven't changed a bit. It's a matter of working only with the best, from people to equipment. Having you on board will be a huge asset for the company."

The company, right. The reminder that he was set in his habits settled her more than anything else he might have said. When they'd met, his expensive tastes were obvious early on, but it had been his common sense, creative problem solving and grounded nature that won her over. "Do you ever drive yourself anymore?"

"Sure. This is better for working." As if on cue, his phone rang. "Excuse me, I need to take this."

She caught sight of a sly blonde on the screen and recognized the picture of Trisha, his current "calendar manager." Sitting beside him, Lucy couldn't avoid overhearing Rush's side of the conversation. Trisha didn't sound too happy with the way her day was going.

Rush's answers became increasingly clipped, his tone terse as the conversation continued. Having seen him in action, Lucy knew Trisha's protests about being moved to a different department were only working against her. Rush didn't tolerate simpering, clingy women and having to repeat himself was a particular pet peeve. The woman's time with Rush would be cut short if she didn't respect the hard limits he put on his personal life.

Mentally, Lucy aimed a string of curses at Kathrein. How many lives would be irreparably altered by his demands? She was tempted to interrupt and explain everything to Rush—until the pictures from the reporter's accident flashed through her mind. Veering from Kathrein's instructions would put Gwen and Jackson in more danger.

She slid a glance at Rush from behind her sunglasses and told herself he'd find a way to mitigate the problems she was about to create.

He ended the call, though Trisha's voice rattled on. "My apologies," he said.

Her stomach cramped with anxiety. She'd never enjoyed causing someone trouble. "If hiring me interferes with—"

He cut her off with a sharp look as the driver pulled to a stop in front of her hotel. "She'll get over it." He shrugged. "Or not. Right now, I don't care."

She worked to keep her mouth closed, to smother the truth of her purpose as she got out of the car and withdrew her keycard.

"I'll wait for you here," he said as they entered the lobby.

She was grateful for the reprieve. The past few hours proved she wasn't even close to being over Rush. All the little things she'd loved about him were still there, tempting her to give in to his invitation to revive their relationship. She couldn't let herself fall back down that rabbit hole, not when her return was based on a lie. On top of that, he was with someone else and she refused to be the other woman.

Alone in her room she swore, vowing impossible retribution on Kathrein as she packed up the few items she'd pulled from her suitcase before meeting Rush at his office. She reached for her laptop and saw the corner of a paper caught between the monitor and keyboard. Carefully, she fished it out and her blood turned to an icy sludge in her veins.

"We await news of your interview." The statement captioned a grainy color picture printed on plain copy paper of her and Rush having lunch.

Cold, her hands quaking, Lucy spun around, as if whoever had been here would suddenly appear.

Asking how he'd managed this was pointless. She should have expected Kathrein to have someone following her, verifying she didn't involve the authorities. Anger revved up and chased the cold from her skin. The creaky old man better stay far away when she was reunited with Gwen and Jackson because if Lucy ever saw him again she'd rip him apart with her bare hands.

She folded the paper in half and tucked the note deep into a document pocket in her laptop bag. After one last sweep of the room, she headed downstairs with her luggage. At the front desk she discovered Rush had paid the bill.

She wheeled on him, her temper seeking the nearest available target. "That wasn't necessary," she said, biting each word. "Get a refund so I can take care of it properly."

"No."

"Yes." She planted her feet and gripped the handle of her suitcase to keep from lunging at him. "I'm neither helpless nor in need of your charity."

His gaze skimmed over the lobby behind her. "Can we discuss this in the car?"

Of course the most eligible bachelor in the city wouldn't want to make a scene in the middle of a hotel. She forced herself to take a breath, to be rational. A public argument would undermine her determination to impact his life as little as possible. She relented, struggling for composure. "Sorry."

He cautiously reached out and took the luggage from her. With her suitcase and laptop bag stowed in the trunk, she slid into the backseat and he followed, nudging her across. "That wasn't a challenge to your independence," he murmured.

She folded her arms over her chest. "I disagree."

"What is the real issue?" He shifted, one arm stretched along the seat back, his fingertips close enough to brush her shoulder if he chose. "You weren't prone to tantrums before."

"This isn't a tantrum." She scooted as far from him as the car allowed, her gaze on the city passing by. "This is resistance to you stepping in and just handling things for me. I'm your personal assistant, remember? Not the other way around."

"Starting tomorrow. Today you're my friend."

She could hardly confess that his thoughtfulness made it harder to deceive him. "Friends don't just pay a friend's hotel bill," she pointed out. "I'm not broke, Rush." No, she was only breaking from the emotional pressure.

"Fine." He withdrew to his side of the seat. "I'll have payroll take it out of your first check."

"Thank you." She hid her misery behind a gracious smile. His solution might have made her happy if this new job was as real as he believed it to be. She supposed she could leave a check with Melva when this was over.

They didn't speak again until they reached the boathouse. The driver pulled into the garage and waited as Rush carried her bags upstairs. Inside, the space held an empty, stale chill, confirming he'd moved out. He walked to the sliding glass door over-looking the yacht harbor and stood there, his back to her, tension radiating from his shoulders.

At last he turned around, but he didn't smile. "A grocery delivery is scheduled. It should be here in a few hours."

"You said you didn't live here."

His gaze drifted around the space. "I don't. I made the call while you were packing up."

"I see."

His inscrutable gaze locked on her suddenly. "I wonder about that." He toyed with his sunglasses. "There's a thing tonight I can't change, or we'd have dinner together."

"I'll be fine on my own." The solitude would be a welcome relief after the travel and whirlwind day.

His chest rose and fell on a big sigh. "Did I ever tell you your independence is attractive?"

She snorted, clapping a hand over her mouth too late to smother the sound. "Not once."

"I should have mentioned it." His smile was wide and easy again, putting a spark in his cornflower-blue eyes. "Make yourself at home. I'll have the most efficient car available delivered later." He winked. "If you don't like it, just let me know when you get to the office."

"Great." She was done arguing about his generosity. He'd just given her the one thing she needed, an evening alone to try and break into the deceased Garmeaux's box. "What time should I be in?" she asked as Rush opened the door to leave.

"Melva is always there first," he said with a wry smile. "I asked her to have the office ready for you by eight."

With that settled, Lucy thanked him once more and closed the door. Much as he'd done, she turned her gaze to the boats and the sunlight sparkling along the dark water of the bay. She'd missed this. The view, the ideal address and homey space outfitted with luxurious finishes, the scent of the water and crisp ocean air that provided a deep counterpoint to the masculine scent and energy of Rush that saturated every corner.

Not anymore. The house had obviously been unoccupied for some time and the only fragrance was the trace of cleaning products. Telling herself that was for the best, she carried her suitcase upstairs to the bedrooms. She stopped short at the doorway to the master. It looked exactly the same as when she'd shared it with Rush, with the king-size bed sprawling across dark hardwood floors and the sleek furniture softened by soft white and nautical blue fabrics.

Troubled, she turned down the hall to the guest suite. If Rush found out and asked about her decision, she'd lean on his theory of a family visit and claim the master had more room for her sister and the baby.

She closed her eyes on a wave of guilt. She had to stay positive, had to believe all three of them would make it through this. Four, if she counted Rush. After quickly unpacking to complete the charade in case there was a visit from a housekeeper in the next few days, she headed back downstairs.

Feeling like an interloper in a space Rush had created for himself, Lucy set up her laptop on the traditional polished-oak desktop in the sleek home office. When everything was connected properly, she turned on the device and soaked up the view of the Golden Gate Bridge while she waited for her system to boot up.

Taking a seat in the black leather chair still adjusted to accommodate Rush's taller frame, she opened her email. The contract from Gray Box was there, along with the new-employee handbook and other documents she should deal with.

The handbook made her smile. She was proud of everything Rush had accomplished, dragging himself from his stint in juvenile detention to these stunning heights. If there was a silver lining in this dreadful situation Kathrein had created, it was the privilege of seeing Rush content and happy and completely in his element as an industry leader.

An instant message window flashed open on her screen and she frowned at the unfamiliar name. A progress report is required.

Kathrein. As if the note in her hotel room hadn't been bad enough. Lucy hunched her shoulders against the trickle of fear sliding down her spine.

Are your guests safe? She typed into the chat window.

Report first.

She sighed. He had the leverage and they both knew it. I am working on it, she replied.

You are wasting time, his next message warned.

As she was typing in her response, a picture popped into the window. Jackson smiled, perched on Kathrein's knee. It looked as if they were a perfectly innocent grandfather and grandson until Lucy noticed the man standing behind Kathrein, holding a menacing black gun aimed casually at the baby's head.

Her eyes welled with tears and her breath caught in her throat. Her fingers fumbled, but she managed to save the picture for later study, hoping to find a clue to their location. Knowing questions about Gwen wouldn't be answered and pleas for mercy wouldn't sway Kathrein, she told him what he wanted to hear and prayed she could make it happen.

You'll get the files.

Waste no more time. Another picture appeared, this time of her and Rush facing off in the hotel lobby.

She rubbed away the rash of goose bumps that raced over her arms with this additional proof Kathrein's man had been trailing her all day, well within striking distance. She couldn't continue to be so naive and oblivious. How had she not noticed?

The chat window disappeared and Lucy raced for the half bath down the hall, her stomach no match for the stress of his vile threats. When the heaving stopped, she sat back on her heels and let the tears flow.

Standing on wobbly legs, she splashed water on her face and rinsed her mouth, then she went back to the office and set to work to save her family.

Chapter Four

Thursday, December 17, 7:20 a.m.

Rush managed to reach the executive floor ahead of Melva and had the coffee brewing when she walked in. "Good morning," he said as he continued work at Trisha's—Lucy's, he reminded himself—desk.

The older woman stopped short, staring at him through the glass walls. "You're early today," she called out.

"First time for everything," he said. "Couldn't sleep," he admitted as he continued clearing the desk before Lucy's arrival.

Melva walked over, her short silver hair styled as perfectly as her subtle makeup. He'd once tried to find out how old she was and been given a runaround he chose not to unravel. Sharp as a tack, she managed the various personalities of the Gray Box top executives with proficiency and kindness.

She wrinkled her nose at the nameplate. "Did you come to your senses about that one?"

And the occasional sharp, maternal touch, Rush added to his list of Melva's attributes. "Trisha has been moved to marketing. A better fit for her skills." He glanced up when Melva sniffed. "What? I thought you'd be thrilled."

"The girl may have a degree, that doesn't give her skills." Melva glanced around. "Why isn't she here taking care of this?"

A question Rush had deliberately stopped asking himself. The answers were too revealing. "I wanted to do it."

Melva pursed her lips. "Knowing how that one was, I figured I'd better come in early to make sure there wasn't a catfight when Lucy arrived."

"Please," he argued. "You're early every day."

She beamed at him with motherly approval. "Hiring Lucy is just what you need."

"She's overqualified to be my assistant." Going on the offensive was the only way to save face.

"Better that than the underqualified string of spokesmodels you've been running through lately." Melva opened a drawer and showed the contents to Rush before dumping everything into the box of personal items on the floor. "Look at this mascara, mankiller red lipstick and nail polish. The only job she wants is Mrs. CEO."

"She knew my rules going in. So what if she takes care of herself?" Rush said. "I respect that."

"I take care of myself," Melva corrected. "What she does is different. She's cotton candy and you know it. Pretty on the outside and no substance underneath."

It was tough to defend Trisha, or any of his recent companions, to Melva. "I give her points for sticking it out through the transition."

"Which transition would that be? Out of the executive suite or out of your life?"

Rush ignored this astute comment. Trisha knew he didn't do long term. She'd used him for a career boost and he'd used her as a distraction for the media. It was a functional system and it sounded better than calling her an emotional crutch. It had been mutual and he'd been clear with her about the true nature of their association.

He couldn't even define his time with Trisha as a relationship. That term had been eliminated from his vocabulary when Lucy walked out on him. Or maybe he'd never truly owned the term. Rush clenched his teeth as the familiar ache pulsed through his system. He'd promised Lucy anything personal between them would be at her request. It might have been the dumbest promise of his life.

His persistent attraction to her defied all logic, all common sense. She'd *left* him and he'd never quite been able to hate her for it. He'd been ready to propose, unaware that she'd been ready to move on. His bruised pride had been nothing compared to the overwhelming sense of loss.

Yesterday he should have sent her packing, yet he'd welcomed her into his business. Eagerly, damn it. He was settling for the smallest crumbs she might toss his way, yet he couldn't stop himself, giving her the job, the boathouse and a car. All of it despite the secrets she was keeping. Throughout his dinner obligations last night he couldn't shake it off, couldn't keep his thoughts away from Lucy. She was back and he wanted to keep her right here where he could enjoy her every day.

He wanted to find a way to get her back into his bed, where he could enjoy her every night, as well. To do that, he'd have to make Melva's day and extricate himself from any perceived personal ties to Trisha.

"Trisha will find someone in marketing to latch on to. It will be better all around."

Melva's pewter eyebrows arched, her gaze full of skepticism. She reached into the box and flipped open a notebook. Rush leaned closer, cringing at the looping handwriting and heart-shaped doodles filling the page.

Mrs. Grayson.

Mrs. Rush Grayson.

Mr. and Mrs. Grayson.

Mrs. Trisha Grayson.

Well, she had excellent penmanship. He groaned. "She knew better. I was clear."

"*You* knew better," Melva scolded.

"I never gave her a reason to think long term was an option with me," he said, putting the lid on the box.

"Hmm, I don't need three guesses why," Melva replied. She hefted the box that contained every last remnant of Trisha's time in the assistant's office.

"Let me get that," Rush said.

"It isn't heavy." Melva shook her head and turned. "I'm only stowing it under my desk for now."

He knew better than to argue when she used that tone. With the desk clear, he sat down to deal with the computer, searching out any files or records Trisha might have added that Lucy wouldn't need. Finding a mocked-up wedding invitation, he sat back in shock. The file had been created yesterday afternoon after he'd messaged Trisha to set up preliminary list of locations for the summer camps.

He should thank Lucy. Her unexpected appearance had helped him dodge a major bullet. Rush scrubbed a hand over his face and deleted the project from the desktop along with several other inappropriate items. Maybe he should just give Lucy a new computer to start fresh. He didn't need to hide his personal life from her. There were always mentions and pictures of him online at gossip sites and in the society pages of the local papers. He hadn't been a monk in her absence, he just hadn't been happy.

The thought jolted him. Of course he was happy. He'd propelled his company to the top and made Gray Box the platinum standard of cloud storage security. His personal life entertained him and served a purpose. He didn't need a serious, meaningful relationship for fulfillment.

So, what was his problem?

He powered down Trisha's system and unplugged everything. Only the monitor would stay. With a text message, he ordered the hardware and software packages Lucy would need and arranged to have them delivered as soon as possible.

He might only have her on a professional level as a personal assistant, but he could be patient and creative about reaching his ultimate goals. What they'd shared was special, even if he hadn't expressed himself well at the time. Their history gave him some excellent ideas about tempting her back into an intimate relationship.

It was five minutes before eight when the elevator doors parted and Lucy appeared. She seemed relaxed as she greeted Melva. Today's dress was a deep sapphire blue. The color reminded him of the water of Wineglass Bay in Australia when he and Gray Box cofounder, Sam Bellemere, had visited several months ago as part of a private consulting gig.

Her hair spilled over her shoulders and her heels clicked softly on the marble floor. As she approached he found himself inadvertently cataloging all the differences between her and Trisha. From the smile to the shoes, the women were night and day. Lucy's smile was confident and open, though at the moment she seemed a little shy, as if he might rescind his offer. Trisha's smile most often appeared with a calculating gleam in her eyes that kept a man on edge. The women were built differently, Trisha tall and slim while Lucy's shorter frame boasted lush curves that had filled his hands. Lucy had a thing for shoes, he knew, but Trisha's spiked heels could have been registered as weapons.

Lucy paused at the door. "Good morning."

Rush shoved his hands into his pockets to keep from grabbing at her and scaring her off. "Welcome to your first day at Gray Box. Has HR been in contact?"

Her smile widened. "I went through as many training units as possible last night. Whoever designed those for you did a thorough job."

"Thanks." Had he ever hired less than the best for any task? His gaze skimmed the desk that was Lucy's now, an obvious contradiction. Well, he had the best person in his assistant's post now and that's what mattered. "A new computer will be here soon." He stepped back and opened his office door. "Once you're settled, grab a coffee and come see me. We'll use this morning to get you up to speed."

"Sounds good." She stowed her purse and a slim laptop bag in the cabinet behind her desk. "I'm ready."

"You didn't bring anything to personalize the space?" With an effort, he suppressed a flare of anger. Was she marking time with him again? He wouldn't tolerate it.

Her gaze dropped to the clean, spacious surface of the desk. "I, *um*…" She cleared her throat. "Most of my belongings are in storage, as I said. I wasn't exactly sure where you would have space for me," she finished.

Her hesitation and obvious scramble for a valid reason irritated him as much as the lack of personal details. There must be someone else in her life, another man she didn't want him to know about.

"Has your working routine changed?" she asked.

"What do you mean?"

"I remember you being single-minded at the office. I'll keep up with you during office hours and personalize the space on my own time."

He deserved the polite pushback. Maybe it had been too long since he'd had a serious employee in this role. He gave in and pressed his fingers to the tension in his neck. "You're right. That hasn't changed." When he dug into a project, he didn't stop until he could call it done and perfect. With plenty of tasks here at the office, she didn't need to know he'd labeled *her* his next primary mission.

"Shall we?" She tilted her head, her hair swaying over her shoulder. He wanted to believe she'd left it down today for him.

"Sure." He led her into his office and switched on the privacy glass. This time he moved to his desk. "Would you rather have pen and paper or an electronic tablet?" he asked. He'd anticipated her answer, torturing himself with another round of the mental game of how well he knew her.

"Tablet, please."

A point for him, he thought, handing her the device. "It's preloaded for Gray Box employees with typical apps, and a guest username and password." He gave her those details. "You can personalize it—"

"On my own time," she finished his sentence with a bright smile.

Frustration rode him hard that she could so effectively behave as if they'd never been more than friends. "Did you sleep well last night?"

She did a double take. "Yes, thank you."

"Good." Wrenching his mind away from the last time he'd seen her in that king-size bed, her dark hair spilling over the white linens, he started to explain how he set his calendar when his office door opened.

He stood up, stifling an oath as Trisha sauntered in, her long legs quickly devouring the distance until she was pressed against him in a hug far too personal for the office. "The privacy glass is on," he said, barely keeping his irritation at bay.

She flicked that away with her white-tipped fingernails. "Oh, I know that doesn't apply to me, darling." Her gaze raked over Lucy, that calculating smile in full force.

"Trisha, let me introduce Lucy Gaines. She'll be taking over as my personal assistant."

He shouldn't have been surprised by Lucy's gracious and warm greeting. Trisha, conversely, was clearly put out. He'd been sure they'd settled this privately.

"A pleasure," Trisha replied.

He nudged Trisha back a step, closer to the door. They'd discussed the camp locations and her move to marketing following last night's dinner at the mayor's house. He refused to allow her to throw a fit here after being so accommodating last night. Her goals of becoming a Mrs. CEO aside, she knew he didn't do personal drama.

"I just need a minute with Rush," Trisha said to Lucy in a tone so sweet his teeth ached. "If you'll excuse us."

"Of course," Lucy replied. "HR just sent me a text message," she added, raising the tablet. "I'll be back as soon as you're ready for me."

He watched Lucy depart, exemplifying the discretion of a valuable PA. "The privacy glass was on, Trisha." It was the safest thing he could say.

"I noticed. Moving me to marketing is bad enough," she pouted. "I only came up here to get my *Rush* for the day." Her fingers trailed along his shirt collar as she giggled over her pun.

"Trisha." He sank into his chair and held her back when she tried to perch on his knee. "You have a communications degree."

She fluttered her eyelashes at him, waiting expectantly for him to continue.

"Marketing is lucky to have you. You knew that desk outside my office wasn't permanent."

The flirty maneuvers ceased instantly. "Who is she, Rush?"

How could he safely answer? "A colleague," he hedged. "She has connections I need to secure some key contracts for us."

"*Us* has a nice ring to it." She tried to capture his hand with hers.

He'd meant it as a company-wide *us*. An unwelcome image of Trisha's "Mrs." doodles flashed through his mind. He resented that he'd have to speak with her about that later, not on company time. "Go have a terrific first day with the marketing team."

"Okay." She bent to kiss him, taking her time so he had a good view of her cleavage. Rush turned and she caught his cheek. Standing tall, she studied him for a long minute before her expression cleared. "Don't work too hard," she said, sashaying out the door.

When the door closed behind her, Rush used a remote at his desk to lock it. He needed a few minutes to get his head on straight. He might have more expertise with technology—and with good reason—but Trisha's possessive signals were inappropriate. Their deal had been for her to be affectionate in public. She'd never pulled a stunt like this at the office. Hearing Melva's warnings in his head, he wished there was a way to convince the older woman to set Trisha straight on his behalf.

He nearly laughed. Melva managing his personal mistakes was less likely than him making any woman a Mrs. Grayson. Between the bad example of his past and his big vision for the future, he wasn't cut out for a conventional marriage and the baggage that came along with it.

He'd packed away the ugliness of his childhood at sixteen, when he'd been busted for hacking, yet those images slid through his mind now. Countless fights over money had ended with slamming doors and his mother's tears, and nothing ever changed. The overtime and weekend shifts, the incessant nagging had divided his parents and pushed Rush deeper into the unfailing logic of computers and code.

People talked about the concept of love as if it was tangible, but he'd never been able to see it. Most people didn't see the programs and code powering their lives, but that was real; it drove operations and made a difference. He sure as hell had never seen love function enough to help anyone. Actions made a difference. *Love* was just another cheap word.

Lucy had been the one woman who'd made him reconsider life as a permanent bachelor. Strong-willed and independent, she'd accepted him as he was. She'd given him space to think and work, and she didn't complain if he interrupted a kiss to jot down an idea. She'd agreed with his assessment that messy emotions ruined a great sexual relationship.

He wanted to reclaim that magic. Surely he could find a way to make her want him again, too. More than his lust for her body, he valued her partnership, affection and unconditional understanding. He didn't believe anyone else could give her the same devotion and satisfaction.

ARMED WITH HER TABLET, Lucy left the executive floor and headed downstairs to HR while Rush shared a private moment with Trisha. The tabloids hadn't done the woman justice, amping up the glam and minimizing the shark factor.

In those few seconds, Rush's girlfriend had painted a clear picture about how they spent time out of the office. Lucy chided herself for letting that little scene bother her. Since she still cared for the man and wanted what was best for him, shouldn't his happiness make her happy, too?

She had no right to feel hurt or cast aside by Rush. She'd made the decision to leave him *after* he'd kept her waiting at a restaurant one too many times. A little voice in her head wondered if he was more careful with personal endeavors now. Based on the evidence Trisha presented, it seemed so.

Lucy shook off the misplaced jealousy. She wouldn't be here long—she only had today and four more to satisfy Kathrein's demands—but she wanted the office staff to know she had the brains to do the job right. Being lumped into the same category as his recent arm-candy assistant would crush her pride.

Keeping a low profile was smarter, yet the more she knew about the office and staff, the better her chances of getting the information for Kathrein. Last night she'd made too many incorrect attempts on the journalist's Gray Box and the system had locked her out. She'd painted herself into a corner and had to hope she could break in through a weakness on the administration side.

Having checked in with HR, she stopped by the other departments, all except marketing. Lucy asked several questions of the small team dedicated to providing tech support to the office. At the encouragement of the department manager, she took a plate of holiday snacks back upstairs to Melva.

When she returned to the executive floor, Rush's office was still frosted with the privacy glass. All the details he'd implemented or invented to make this building state-of-the-art impressed her. Under different circumstances, working here—in a capacity other than his assistant—might well have been her dream job.

Melva hopped up the minute she saw the covered plate. "Is that from Joey in IT?"

Lucy nodded, smiling through another wave of sadness. Melva would be disappointed in her when the deception was exposed.

"That boy loves me, praise God. Have you had a taste?"

"Not yet."

"Well, bring over a chair and prepare for addiction."

Melva peeled back the plastic wrap covering the plate and they dug into the sweet, colorful holiday treats while Melva walked Lucy through the corporate calendar program and explained how Rush typically scheduled his time. She blotted her lips with a napkin. "I'll introduce you to the others since his highness is still tied up," Melva said.

An unwelcome image of Rush tied up and defenseless against Trisha's blatant sexuality popped into Lucy's mind. Her cheeks heated, remembering the first time they'd played with blindfolds and handcuffs in what had been a phenomenal night of pleasure.

"You don't need to worry that they'll write you off as another useless Trisha," Melva was saying. "They'll see you for who you are."

Just like old times, Melva could read her mind. This time, Lucy hoped the older woman was wrong. She was here to crack open a Gray Box, and if word of that breach got out the company would suffer.

But was there any way of doing what she had to do without the world finding out?

Don't think about the consequences. Do what you have to do.

Melva introduced her to the chief financial officer, Ken Lawrence, as well as Torry Harrison, currently the vice president of research and development. She shook hands with both men, silently commending Rush for acquiring superb talent.

"I know who you are," Torry said, a smile wreathing his face. "Rush used to quote you all the time in meetings."

Lucy blushed for a far more appropriate reason this time. "He mentioned you and your innovative outlook during a lecture when I was in grad school. It's a pleasure to finally put a face to the name." After Gray Box had locked her out last night, she'd spent the rest of her evening reading up on all of the senior staff, telling herself that was what any responsible assistant would do.

"Will you join Rush at the fund-raiser tonight?" Ken asked.

"Oh, I haven't heard about that yet," she replied, glancing at Melva for help.

"Rush adopted the children's hospital expansion as a pet project." Melva fanned her face. "He booked the Palace," she finished with a reverent whisper.

"That sounds lovely," Lucy said. She could imagine the glamour of Trisha and Rush emerging from a limo and strolling through the indulgent grandeur of the restored building.

"The open bar is the real perk," Torry joked. "As his new assistant, you should be there. Everyone else from Gray Box is going. The place is sure to be packed with people who might be assets or allies in the future. You could network and lay some groundwork. My wife and I can pick you up."

She floundered for a polite excuse, knowing she didn't have suitable formal wear with her or the time to shop. On top of that, with someone tailing her for Kathrein, she didn't dare do anything he might interpret as wasting time.

"Stop it, Torry. He's being ornery," Melva interjected. "He just wants to one-up Rush and arrive in style with two beautiful women."

Lucy laughed. "I think I'll have to pass tonight.

Maybe next year." If everyone was going, she'd have the office to herself. It was the opening she needed.

"What would be even better," Torry said, "is getting your opinion on our latest ideas."

She caught Melva's encouraging smile. "Why me?" Lucy asked. "I don't even have a full day to my credit yet." She didn't want to like everyone so much. Even Trisha had the singular redeeming quality of marking Rush as off-limits—something Lucy needed to keep at the front of her mind.

"As I said, Rush talked about you a great deal. I think your perspective on this is just what I need to clarify our branding."

Her tablet chimed and she saw a message from Rush that he was ready for her again. "Can I take a rain check? The boss is calling."

"The man has a sixth sense." Torry shrugged, shooting her a wry smile. "Come see me this afternoon if he gives you some breathing space."

"Sure thing." Lucy hurried away and gave Rush a quick wave through the clear glass as she approached.

"I appreciate your patience," Rush said as she resumed her place in one of the chairs in front of his big desk. "Trisha—"

She cut him off. "You don't have to explain a thing." She couldn't handle any details. If Rush claimed nothing was going on between him and Trisha, Lucy's hormones would wreck her concentration, and if he said things were serious between them she'd be heartbroken all over again. "My job is to assist you and that means adjusting my schedule to yours."

"Okay." He pushed up the sleeves of his black sweater. "What did Torry have to say?"

"Oh." She glanced back over her shoulder. "Melva made introductions," she said. "He mentioned the fund-raiser tonight."

Rush rolled his eyes. "Yeah."

"I noticed it isn't on your calendar."

"I tend to leave off the events I don't want to attend," he admitted. "Especially those scheduled for after hours."

"That kind of habit makes it easy to overbook you." She typed it into the calendar and he groaned when it appeared on his computer monitor. "Melva says this fund-raiser is important to you. A new pet project—her words. Why don't you want to go?"

"I have a new project on my mind, but I do need to be there tonight," he finished. "Now, are we all synced up?"

She reviewed the calendar on her tablet. "I guess we'll find out over the next few days." Despite the fact that he was a recluse, it had taken her almost a week to get all of Kathrein's appointments organized so everyone in the household and office knew what was happening. Although he rarely traveled, people frequently came to his estate or sought meetings by video conference.

Rarely traveled. Her mind stuck on that one point. Kathrein had sent those pictures to torture her, but also to prove he had Jackson. It was a stretch to think he'd separated mother and son. That meant he had to be holding them somewhere close to his house. Or not. Kathrein had three properties she knew of in Europe and she had to assume he had more hideaways scattered around the globe. With his private jet, he could be anywhere and move his hostages at any moment.

"Lucy?"

"Hmm?" She yanked her attention back to the far-more-handsome billionaire in front of her. "Yes, we're synced up. Sorry, my mind wandered."

"Nowhere pleasant," Rush observed. "All that tension is back. Are you sure you're okay?"

She smiled so fast she thought her face might split. "Of course. Yesterday you outlined responsibilities that went beyond calendar management and screening your calls. Can you tell me why the phone at my desk doesn't ring?"

He cleared his throat. "Melva is in the habit of handling the calls."

"She and I can make that change right away. What about the other items?"

He smiled, but there was a weary regret in his

eyes. "Tomorrow. Talk with Melva about the calls and go ahead and chat with Torry. He could use your insight."

"All right." She was at the door when he stopped her with one more order.

"And put something personal on your desk by the end of the day."

He'd practically growled the demand and her body reacted with a fervent sizzle. She turned and gave him a cheery smile, hiding the reaction. "You're the boss."

Chapter Five

Rush had better things to do than watch Lucy work through the glass that separated their offices. Unfortunately, he couldn't keep his mind on any of them. More than once he'd reached for the switch to apply the privacy glass and couldn't do it. Having her back, having her right there within view—if not quite within reach—played havoc with his mind.

Only a fool would be distracted with the worry that she'd disappear again if he took his eyes off her, yet he couldn't shake the feeling that her return wasn't permanent.

It was their ugly history, he told himself more than once as the day wore on. His bruised pride over the way she'd left him before. He was competitive and he'd lost her. The failure didn't sit well.

A message window popped up in the corner of his desk monitor. It was a direct message from Sam in the security department asking Rush to trek down to the basement for a meeting.

Irritable, he glanced again toward Lucy's desk. Her computer had been delivered and he knew she was getting up to speed with the company systems. She'd apparently ignored his instruction to personalize her space. Would it be a picture of her sister and nephew or maybe a trinket from France? God help him if she put up a picture of herself with another man.

He stood, took two steps toward Lucy and then abruptly turned on his heel, choosing to use his private access to get downstairs. He had a company to run and yet he'd spent last night searching every possible media outlet for some new detail on Lucy's personal life. The fact that she'd worked with an aging recluse didn't help his cause. He had no problem using his substantial resources to keep tabs on her, but it was aggravating that she'd managed to keep her personal life a secret. He'd never figure out how to win her back if he didn't know who else was on the playing field.

Entering the security offices from the stairwell, he took a moment to just appreciate all they'd accomplished. At one time, he'd been a kid on the other end of a computer connection, breaching firewalls and protective algorithms far weaker than those Gray Box employed now.

As he walked toward Sam's workspace, he couldn't suppress the sense of pride in their accomplishments. He and Sam had met in juvenile detention, both serving time for cyber crimes against government agencies. Now, still friends and equal partners in business, they were entertaining requests from government agencies worldwide for the proprietary and far superior security systems they'd developed.

"What's so sensitive you won't use the company email, Sam?" Rush waited while his friend's fingers flew over the keyboard, his face lit by the glow from the multiple-monitor array.

At last Sam sat back, cracking his knuckles. "It's subtle and I'm still tracking things down, but I think someone out there is taking a shot at us," he replied with a grin.

Attacks were fairly common, considering Gray Box was the pinnacle of cloud-based security. Hackers who resembled Rush and Sam in their youth frequently tried to break the unbreakable Gray Box. The person who succeeded would have bragging rights within the shadow community for life.

Rush studied the screens, though the pattern wasn't clear to him. "Have you picked up a code trail?"

"No." Sam scowled at the center monitor.

"Were they taking a crack at specific boxes? Our big clients aren't exactly confidential."

"That would be near impossible to figure out." Sam eyed him over his square black-framed glasses, his lip curled in disgust. "That kind of thing is beneath my paygrade. We have countless forgotten-password lockouts every day. Hell, every hour of every day."

"Then why haul me down here?" Rush propped a hip on the edge of the desk.

"There was an attempt on the main system through an admin access," Sam replied.

"Doesn't that happen every day, too?"

"Not on old backdoor usernames." Sam's mouse circled code on another screen.

Rush listened attentively to Sam's explanation. Subtle was definitely the right word if this was an attack and not another standard poke at the bear. "We haven't used that goofy name on anything current have we?"

"Of course not. We retired it as an outdated antique."

Rush stood up and rocked back on his heels. As fast as their tech business advanced, a term, an approach, even a username could be rendered useless in less than a year. This particular admin name had been one they'd used as kids when they'd left back doors open for later access. Still, among those with a hacker mindset, especially a young hacker mindset, it wasn't impossible to come up with that character combination.

Sam leaned back in his chair, fingers drumming on the armrests. "Did you fire anyone lately?"

"Not anyone capable of this."

"So the latest assistant didn't have any tech skills?" Sam wiggled his eyebrows. "She had great legs."

"I didn't fire her, I moved her to marketing." Trisha didn't qualify as jilted and she definitely didn't have tech skills. Per their original agreement, he'd set her up with a job that suited her and since they were attending tonight's gala fund-raiser together, they'd still be seen as a couple by the media. "What about you?" He turned the tables on Sam. "Any boastful pillow talk lately?"

"You're kidding, right?" Sam sat up straight, throwing an arm wide to encompass the aisles and aisles of servers behind him. "You're the only one who gets out of the office enough to have a social life."

Rush laughed. It was an old joke. Sam, terminally shy, preferred to keep a computer screen between him and his romantic liaisons. Not even the fortunes they'd amassed and invested seemed to give his friend much confidence in social settings. "Come to the fund-raiser and I'll introduce you to someone."

"No, thanks. I don't need your weepy castoffs," Sam joked. He surged forward and tried another search, sat back disappointed again. "Have you pissed off anyone lately?"

"I piss off people every day," Rush admitted. "No one comes to mind as a possible culprit."

"Fine," Sam said with a resigned sigh. "This bugs

me enough that you needed to know. I'll keep working at it and see if anything pops open."

"Thanks. I'll mull it over and let you know if I think of anyone who might use that name."

Sam nodded absently, his fingers already tapping out more commands on the keyboard. They were a pair. Rush might be the face of Gray Box, but Sam was the virtual muscle and together they were the top minds in software and development. If there was a problem on the horizon, they'd root it out and take appropriate action.

Back upstairs in his office, Rush switched gears and reviewed notes from his recent talks at local schools. Had he inadvertently used that backdoor name as a part of his example? If so, it would've been the first time.

While he always gave a quick background explanation of the cocky hacker kid he'd been, and his stint in juvie because of his mistakes, he never dwelled on it or gave up information that could be used as a guide to send a kid down the wrong path. Usually he focused on the creativity, team effort and hard work that had eventually made Gray Box a household name.

When he was satisfied that he hadn't inadvertently planted ideas in the head of an ambitious youngster, he returned to the other items on his agenda. He really wanted the contract with the company he'd walked out on yesterday morning. Considering the sensitive nature of the Family Services offices, the information security package he'd presented should have been a no-brainer.

Yes, the holiday season was a tough time to wrap up that kind of deal. On the flip side, Rush knew they were still in the first quarter of their fiscal year and he wanted a slice of that security upgrade budget. He drafted a snarky email making it clear they could contract his company to do it right or they could contract him later to fix the inevitable mess.

Reading it through he knew his lawyers would have a collective heart attack if he sent it, so he deleted it and started over. The second draft was worse than the first, so he shoved back from his desk. Pacing the width of his spectacular view of San Francisco, he fought to corral his fragmented thoughts.

At the soft rapping on his door, he turned hoping to see Lucy. *Not my day*, he thought, waving Trisha in. Why couldn't the woman stay at her new desk with the marketing team? Behind her, he saw Lucy wasn't at her desk. Was there something about the space that actually repelled his assistants?

"How is your day going?" he asked.

She gave a delicate shrug of one shoulder, setting the silk of her top rippling. "I won't complain." The curt tone and sharp smile set off alarms in his head. "What time will the limo come by tonight?"

"Limo?" Rush spotted Lucy in the conference

room with Torry. They appeared to be discussing a presentation spread across the table. Why just the two of them? The hem of her dress rose just a bit as she leaned over the table and Rush's brain flooded with the memory of her warm, ticklish skin just above and behind her knees. Yes, he'd told her to meet with Torry, but she was *his* personal assistant. She wasn't here to help everyone with a random question. He closed his eyes, willing away the childish jealousy.

"The children's hospital fund-raiser." Trisha snapped her fingers at him. "It is *the* social event this week. Don't even think of ducking it."

"Sure." His gaze remained locked on that conference room where Lucy laughed as Torry grinned. Rush willed himself to get a handle on the surge of jealousy before he did something stupid, like toss Torry out on his ass along with his stock options.

"Rush? Rush!"

"Yes?" He gave Trisha his full attention, but he could see from the temper in her eyes, coloring her cheeks, it was far too late.

"Who is she?"

He met her angry outburst with the cool detachment he relied on when personal attachments turned sticky. "I answered that question last night."

"No," she countered immediately. "You dodged that question." With a toss of her hair, she stomped out of his office and into the space that had been hers only twenty-four hours ago, leaving the door open.

"Come back here." The last thing he wanted was to air this out in front of everyone.

"I won't. You could have shown me the courtesy of being discreet." Her voice, breaking on false emotion, carried through the executive space and heads turned to watch. Lucy's included.

"Trisha," he warned. "Let's discuss this like adults." He tipped his head back to his office. "Please," he added.

"Is this a conquest issue? You just need a challenge?"

"Enough." At the moment, he just wanted her to stop shouting. "This is a silly misunderstanding."

"Silly!" she screeched, throwing up her hands. "Hardly." Snatching a picture frame from Lucy's desk, she shook it at him. "You, God's gift, probably think you can convert her."

"What the hell are you talking about?" Why hadn't he installed privacy glass on the assistant spaces as well? Not that it would help much since only the executive offices and conference rooms had actual doors.

"She'll be the first thing you fail at, you idiot!" The picture frame landed with a thud against his chest and he barely caught it before it tumbled to the floor.

"Trisha, stop."

"No! I quit. That lousy marketing job is beneath

me." She turned up her nose. "And all your charities and community events are boring as hell. You
aren't worth it."

She dashed at her cheeks as if she was crying, but
he was close enough to see her eyes were dry. The
elevator doors opened just as she reached them. He
had to assume Melva had called up the express car.
Trisha flounced off, making a dramatic exit on her
spiked heels.

In the ringing silence that followed, he looked at
the picture in his hands and smiled with relief. Not
a boyfriend. Lucy had personalized her space with
a candid shot of Gwen and Jackson cuddled up in
front of a Christmas tree. Trisha must have assumed
by this that Lucy was gay.

Suppressing a laugh, he replaced the framed picture on Lucy's desk and returned to his office, switch-
ing on the privacy glass. If that was the way Trisha
needed to save her dignity, he'd manage the inevitable
ribbing from his executive team. Having her out of
the offices and out of his life was worth the momentary embarrassment.

Everyone up here had started as his friend and they
all understood the limits of his personal life. Even
Lucy. *Especially Lucy*, he thought with a grimace.

He briefly considered inviting her to attend the
fund-raiser with him and decided it was a bit much to
extend her first day like that. The dark shadows under

her eyes gave away her travel fatigue and he couldn't ask her to come along simply to save his pride.

Besides, with just the one suitcase, he doubted she'd packed anything suitable for a gala. *I travel light.* Somehow those words made him feel worse, although he couldn't pinpoint why.

Usually he worked past six, but not today. He needed to get out of here and get his head together for tonight and he sent Lucy a note that he was going home.

During the short walk to his condo he had a rare flash of regret. Home used to mean the boathouse and evenings with Lucy. Now it was a cold, modern condo with no soul and dinner for one prepared by his personal chef. Trisha was right about one thing— he was an idiot for letting Lucy get away.

He warmed up the food as directed, seriously debating skipping the fund-raiser. It wouldn't be the first time he'd blown off a charity event at the last minute. The guest list would be littered with locals loaded with money and good intentions along with a few celebrities.

Trisha was right about that, too. He couldn't duck out tonight. Rush needed to set the fund-raising bar high enough to make a difference and get the new expansion off the ground. He and Sam had toured the children's cancer ward just last week, bringing the latest video game consoles into the lounge and taking on all challengers. The kids who couldn't make it were able to watch from their rooms and when nurses approved, they'd been able to duel with a few of those isolated patients on handheld systems.

He ate dinner, not really tasting the food. Reluctantly, he pulled together his tuxedo for the gala and shored up his gloomy mood by calling the building valet for his Tesla Roadster. So what if it was the car Lucy's laughter had filled while he'd navigated the seaside cliffs on a hot summer night? He relegated the memory to the back of his mind, along with all the other mistakes and unfixable problems of his past.

Although he could walk or take the limo, he wanted to make a statement. The magnificent lines of the near-silent car earned admiring and curious looks everywhere he went. When he pulled up at the hotel tonight, he wanted all eyes on his solitary arrival.

Life had taught him early the best way to climb out of any difficult situation was to keep moving forward.

Chapter Six

Outside, darkness had fallen over the city and the lights from surrounding buildings twinkled like stars around the Gray Box office. Everyone had gone home and, in the quiet of the empty executive floor, Lucy could hear the clock ticking. Not a real clock; the interior design was too modern for that. No, she heard that incessant ticking in her head and her heart, knowing Gwen and Jackson were running out of time.

Just after lunch she'd received another picture of Kathrein with her nephew. Both Kathrein and Jackson were wearing different clothing and the old man gripped a calendar page with red Xs marking the days she'd lost. The pictures gave Lucy zero reassurance that her family was safe. The armed bodyguard loomed like a vicious shadow in the background. Her demand for a current picture of Gwen remained unanswered.

He'd given her one way out of this. She had to get inside that Gray Box and get out before anyone discovered her breach. Definitely to save Gwen and Jackson, but to protect Rush, as well. Nothing good would come of her return to his life.

His current girlfriend had dumped him, making a public scene Rush surely hated. No matter his flattering words about her having the background and mindset to assist him, once she succeeded in stealing the documents, he'd never forgive her.

Since Kathrein had kidnapped her family and dumped this outrageous task on her, she'd been racking her brain for all the tips and tricks she'd learned while listening to Rush talk about computer security. It couldn't be impossible. The consequences of failure shivered through like a cold wind as she glanced at the picture of her family.

No, she had to believe. Rush had taught her very few things were unbreakable. Despite the Gray Box motto, she knew there had to be a way in. She'd gone as far as possible with direct attempts on the journalist's box and come up empty. Now her only hope was to find a back door or a weaker administration access. She poked and prodded through the system, getting no closer to the documents she needed.

When she'd taken herself on the tour today, she'd met people from several departments and asked questions about the various roles within the company, under the guise of understanding how things meshed and overlapped. The answers gave her insight she intended to use as entry points, but those replies also confirmed that Kathrein should have blackmailed a real hacker. Someone as good as Rush had been before he'd flipped his focus to protecting data.

She dropped her head into her hands and ordered herself to think. Rush had also taught her the value of tenacity. He lived it every day. The man never gave up on a target.

That's why she'd left without a word and faked a new boyfriend in Chicago. That last evening hadn't been the first time he'd stood her up. Rush had been clear from the start that he never planned to shift his remarkable dedication from business to nurture a personal relationship. He wanted physical intimacy and friendship. In turn, she'd never wanted him to change into something he wasn't. It hadn't been his fault she'd broken the rules and fallen for a man who didn't believe in love. He was too perceptive. She'd had to get out on her own terms before he discovered how deep her emotions ran and forced her out of his life.

Frustrated with that useless train of thought, the tick-tick-tick banging in her head, she rocked back in her chair. Swiveling around, she peeked through the glass wall, half expecting Rush to be sitting at his desk. The office was dark and empty, the lights of the city skyline sparkling from the other side of all that glass. Rush always pushed forward with relentless tunnel vision and this unarguable statement of success was the latest proof.

She still admired him for his dedication to improving himself, his work and the community. One night at the boathouse after she'd cooked dinner, he'd reluctantly shown her a picture of himself and Sam as teenagers. It hadn't been long after their release from detention. At sixteen, he'd been rough around the edges, with shaggy black hair and gritty determination in his bold blue gaze. He'd been down on his luck, but she could see he was already looking for a way back into the game.

That candid picture had shown her everything she needed to know about him. A brilliant man with a creative entrepreneurial spirit, he'd hauled himself up and out of that mess and made his first windfall in his early twenties. Maybe she should tell him the truth. If anyone could understand why she was doing the wrong thing for the right reasons, it would be Rush.

If anyone could devise a better solution, it would be him, as well. When they'd been dating and she'd been sincerely frustrated over struggles and aggravations in academic circles as she'd worked on her MBA, his creative, hypothetical solutions ranged from innocent and ornery to complex and dazzling.

This was different. Any deviation from her instructions would have Kathrein taking horrific action against her sister and nephew. Instinctively, she glanced to the exterior windows, wondering who was watching and if they had eyes on her now.

She turned her attention back to the empty office, weighing one lousy option against the next. If she could get into Rush's system, surely the entire company would be at her fingertips. With what amounted to a Gray Box master key, she could find a way to manipulate the settings and access the files Garmeaux had stored here.

Wiping her damp palms on her skirt, she stood up and took a step toward Rush's sanctuary. In the increasingly small world of technology security, if a breach like this came to light, he would be ruined.

"No choice." Speaking aloud muffled that incessant ticking in her head. Gwen and Jackson were all the family she had. And really, who would complain? Rush would be furious but he wouldn't publicize it if she succeeded. Garmeaux was dead. Stealing the files wouldn't tarnish his reputation as a journalist. It wasn't much of a silver lining, but she clung to it.

Lucy's breath shuddered in and out of her lungs as she crossed Rush's office. The carpet felt too plush; the air was imbued with lingering traces of his cologne. She stopped at the corner of his desk as a small voice in her head screamed for her to turn back.

No. When her computer was installed, she'd learned how Rush segmented the hardware and software to suit each facet of the business. Only Rush and Sam, as the head of security, had the ability to delve into any department. She had a much better chance of figuring out Rush's passwords than those of his partner.

She sat down at the desk and laid her fingers on the keyboard. Rush could rebuild a business. During her trek through the offices, she'd seen all sorts of ideas in development. He could rebound from an attack on the company, but her sister and nephew would die if she failed.

With another glance to confirm she was alone on the executive floor, she brought his desktop computer to life. As she fidgeted in the chair, his scent surrounded her. Familiar and enticing, it sparked a new reaction this time—guilt.

Before she'd walked away from Rush as a matter of self-preservation, the masculine fragrance held only sensual, happy memories. She used to fall asleep in that big bed in the boathouse, utterly satisfied and content, wrapped in his strong arms and the enduring deep notes of his favorite cologne warmed by his body. Her muscles went lax as she sat there, her body eager for one more encounter with the man. She'd dared more with him, trusted him in bed and out, more than either of the men she'd been close to before him. And, contrary to the rumors she'd started, she hadn't been with anyone since.

When he discovered her deception, there wouldn't

be a second chance with him in her future. Even if Rush eventually understood her reasons, if she cracked Garmeaux's box and someone else in the company learned about the breach his legal team would insist on prosecuting her. Ignoring the tears stinging her eyes, she set to work in the darkened office, carefully thinking through every keystroke, planning and tracking her attempts with pen and paper.

To her shock, she succeeded on her second login attempt and the reporter's files on Kathrein filled the screen. Her momentary sense of victory was quickly muted by what she had to do for Kathrein. By tomorrow morning, she'd be back on a plane to France for a reunion with her family and Rush would be a permanent part of her past.

THE GALA WAS going exactly as Rush anticipated. Bored and unhappy, he beamed at acquaintances while pretending to sip the champagne on offer. It wasn't his favorite beverage, but it was a far better choice than the open bar, especially with so many women in the room who'd noticed his solitary arrival. Despite his best efforts, his thoughts drifted back to his favorite champagne moment with Lucy at the boathouse. God, what an experience. Her body had always intoxicated him more than any liquor and he struggled to suppress an instant erection at thoughts of sipping ice-cold trails of bubbly from her soft, warm skin.

Since the evening he'd walked in to find the boathouse deserted, he'd tried and failed to purge her from his system. Part of him hated having her back. None of his successes mattered when held up against his stellar failure with her. His subsequent failure to get over her eroded his self-confidence, though he didn't let anyone close enough to notice.

The engagement ring he'd purchased remained in the safe at the boathouse. He'd never had the guts to return it to the jeweler. In fact, he'd never gone back, taking the coward's way out and using other jewelers so he wouldn't have to acknowledge his mistakes with Lucy.

With his society-page smile, he did his part for the fund-raising, shaking hands and issuing friendly challenges to those in attendance to dig into their deep pockets for such a worthy cause. He posed for pictures, ignoring humanity's fickle nature and short memory. Sixteen years ago he'd been in police custody. Tonight, no one seemed bothered that his past exploits as a juvenile delinquent had been an integral foundation for a system they used to preserve and protect information online.

As the jazz ensemble took their second break, he decided he could leave during the next set without raising eyebrows. He scanned the room, wondering about the wisdom of leaving with a beautiful woman on his arm. Though it wouldn't be the first time he sought a one-night stand, tonight it pricked his long-dormant conscience.

He'd rather have Lucy beside him, exchanging knowing looks at the outrageous personal propositions and professional queries he constantly fielded at events like this one. She had a knack for evading pushy people without causing any insult. On top of that she never failed to put him at ease in a crowd whenever he felt that old anxiety of being trapped creep up on him.

As another hospital patron took the stage to eloquently narrate a heart-wrenching story designed to create a tidal wave of donations, Rush's phone vibrated in the inner pocket of his tuxedo jacket. He slipped out of the ballroom to check the alert.

He read the text message from Sam asking if he wanted to split a pizza. What the hell? They often did that when pulling all-nighters during the development stage of a project. Pizza at the office sounded a hell of a lot better than going the distance here at the fund-raiser. He sent a message back, offering to pick up Sam's favorite, black olive and sausage, on his way back.

Back? Thought you were upstairs, came the reply.

Rush started for the valet stand, his stride devouring the expansive lobby as he pressed the button to call Sam's cell phone. "Why do you think I'm upstairs?" he asked when Sam answered.

"Your computer is logged on."

Crap. "Hold on." Rush bounced on his toes as he waited for the valet to bring his car. Sam offered to send security upstairs, but Rush held him off. There was a logical explanation. He tipped the valet and slid into the driver's seat, syncing the phone with the car's stereo speakers. "Is anyone else logged in?" he asked, pulling away from the hotel.

"A few people here and there."

"I mean on the executive floor?" Rush ground his molars until his jaw ached. Silently, the car slid through traffic like quicksilver, pushing the upper edge of the speed limit as well as his luck.

"Oh. Sure. Lucy's system is on," Sam answered after a few seconds.

Rush eased off the accelerator and his pulse slowed as well. "Then no big deal. That's okay."

"How do you figure?"

He didn't know. Off the top of his head, he couldn't think of any reason she would be in his office, much less on his computer. "Just—I don't know—just don't send up security. I'm on the way and I'll talk with her personally."

"If you say so," Sam teased.

"I do." Rush snapped. "Thanks for the heads-up," he added.

"And the pizza?"

Rush laughed. He could always count on Sam to be practical. "Call it in and I'll pick it up." He heard Sam's fingers speeding over his keyboard.

"Order in," Sam said after a few more seconds. "I'm glad we convinced them to upgrade to online ordering."

"Uh-huh." Rush's thoughts were devoted to Lucy and what she was up to when Sam's swearing interrupted his budding theories. "What now?" Rush drummed his fingers on the steering wheel while he waited for a traffic light to change.

"You want the good news first or the bad?"

Rush sighed. "Informant's choice," he replied.

He didn't want any bad news if it pertained to Lucy, but Sam was focused on the data rather than personal sentiment. With any luck, Lucy was using his corporate account to order some indulgent lingerie. Unfortunately for his vivid fantasy life, she wasn't the type of woman to abuse access that way.

"Looks like your new assistant used an older login and went straight for a particular Gray Box."

Aw, hell. Luck wasn't on his side tonight. "She's not in the research and development or financials?"

"No," Sam stretched out the word. "Are you telling me you hired someone you thought *would* breach those areas?"

"Of course not." Lucy wasn't capable of corporate espionage. He didn't believe her capable of using him or his money at all. He slammed the car to a stop in front of the pizza joint. "Don't confront her. Just keep tabs on what she's doing."

Sam groused and swore, but he agreed to let Rush handle it.

Rush picked up the pizza, hiding the turmoil seething under his skin. What the hell was she up to? He returned to the building and carried the pizza straight to Sam's office. "Any update?" He cleared clutter from one corner of Sam's desk and stacked the pizza box, napkins and paper plates there.

"No." Sam tilted his chin to the monitor array. "She's still in that box. Almost an hour now."

Rush couldn't believe she'd managed to fool him. The pain in his gut was worse than the beatings he'd survived in juvie, a complete sucker punch. Rush wasn't sure he'd ever trust anyone but Sam again.

"You'll fire her, right?"

"My assistant, my business," Rush said, taking a bite of pizza.

"Per the usual," Sam grumbled, dragging two big slices onto his plate. "I created a ghost of the box. Whatever her intention is, I'm protecting the client's content."

"Good job." With a nod of appreciation, Rush left his half-eaten pizza slice behind and headed to his private elevator. Lucy had one chance to give him the logical explanation.

Chapter Seven

The ticking clock in Lucy's head fell silent as she read and reread the documents Garmeaux had assembled. The reports and research implied Dieter Kathrein was an imposter. Every startling revelation caused an inescapable dread to pool in her belly. She was up against a man capable of anything, a monster who had killed without any sign of remorse.

In the month she'd been with Kathrein, she'd learned his absolute commitment to family, especially his grandson and only heir to his fortune. The information here would definitely end his grandson's political aspirations and possibly destroy anyone close to him.

Tears rolled down her cheeks as she considered the potential fallout of the terrible secrets Kathrein could never allow to come to light. She transferred the Gray Box contents of old records, articles, interviews and images to a thumb drive and deleted the items from the box one by one. She took a screen shot of the empty box and added it to the files on the thumb drive.

Assuming it was all true, she was now the only other person who knew about Kathrein's awful past. If he honored his deal and spared her sister and nephew, Lucy would be killed. There was no alternative, no other way to keep his grandson safe. Did she have any hope of convincing him she hadn't opened any of it?

How had her ideal job turned into a nightmare?

She heard the chime of the elevator arriving in the private corridor and her heart kicked with a spike of adrenaline. Knowing it had to be Rush didn't bring her any comfort. Yanking the thumb drive from the computer, she hurried to erase her tracks.

She wasn't fast enough.

He hit the office lights, his eyes dark and dangerous as his tall frame filled the doorway. His bow tie was undone, hanging loose, and the top button of the crisp white shirt was open. "Lucy."

Not a query, a statement. He wasn't surprised to find her. She closed her eyes as shame washed over her. Naturally, he'd have some safeguards in place, maybe even hidden cameras to protect his interests. He was the king of modern security, after all.

"I'm sorry," she whispered.

He didn't move or acknowledge her apology.

"It's not what it looks like," she said.

"It looks like you're in my office taking advantage of my absence."

She swallowed back protests and lame excuses. Rush wouldn't tolerate either. She rapidly blinked away more tears, afraid he'd think she was trying to play on his emotions. Emotions he kept locked away as securely as any bit of data in his Gray Boxes. She didn't want to lie to him any more than she already had. "I was working late and I came in here when my own system didn't cooperate." There. She'd given him two truths.

"Lucy." His black eyebrows arrowed up toward his hairline and he leaned against the doorjamb, his arms folded over his wide chest.

She wasn't fool enough to believe the relaxed posture. He was in full predator mode and she was the hapless prey. She shook her head, unable to force out the right lies. "I'll go." She stepped away from his desk.

"You are not dismissed."

His voice was cold, each syllable an icy shard separate from the others. She froze.

"Your previous boss has shown little interest in developing cloud-based security."

Another statement. Lucy willed her feet to move away from his personal space behind the desk. With every second her misery mounted. Rush wasn't a man to easily forgive such an invasion. He smiled for the cameras, knew how to play the game in public to get what and where he wanted, but he valued his privacy. More than once, she'd seen how the publicity took a toll on him. "It's not what it looks like," she repeated.

"Kathrein," he barked. "He put you up to this?"

She glanced toward her desk and the framed photo of her family and straightened her shoulders. "No," she lied.

Eyes narrowed, Rush took a step inside the office. "Then what are you up to?"

Before she could reply, he moved to the desk and snatched up the notepad she had left behind. Damn! Lucy scurried to the opposite side of his desk as he dropped into his chair and set his hands to the keyboard.

"Who is Mathieu Garmeaux?" Rush demanded.

"He's not important," she answered, sticking with the few honest answers she could give. No chance of escape, but she wanted to protect Rush.

"You broke into his box."

She nodded. "He won't file a complaint." One more weak truth that failed to make her feel better. The knots in her stomach pulled tighter. "Really, Rush. Ignore my stupid mistake. Please. I didn't mean to cause trouble. I just… I just…"

"What?" he roared.

The single word caused her entire body to spasm and her resolve shattered like the Christmas ornaments left behind in the manor house in France. Her knees wobbled; a dark haze crowded her vision. She sagged into the nearest chair before she passed out. "I had to do it," she said, ignoring the tears rolling down her cheeks. "Kathrein is holding Gwen and Jackson hostage." She gulped in air and choked on a sob. "He demanded the documents and information from that box in exchange for their lives."

On a dark oath Rush came around the desk and pulled her up into his arms. He smelled like expensive perfume, spicy tomato sauce and there, underneath it all, the man she loved. She burrowed closer, her hands sliding up his back under his jacket and her tears soaking the fabric of his tuxedo shirt.

"I'm so sorry," she mumbled into his chest. "He didn't give me an option, but now I know the truth and—" Panicked hiccups cut off her explanation.

"Easy." Rush rubbed a hand up and down her spine. "Breathe."

She relaxed under his soothing touch, sighing as he freed her hair of the clip that had held it up since dinnertime. "Garmeaux is—was a reporter, Rush." She gripped his lapels. "He's dead. Kathrein had him killed. I'm sure of it now that I've seen the files." She struggled to get the words out around the lump of fear lodged in her throat. "Even if he releases Gwen and Jackson, his only choice is to kill me, too."

His muscles went rigid at her words and then relaxed again. "Shh." He cupped her face in his hands and stroked away her tears with his thumbs. "Slow down." His blue eyes were full of tenderness and longing as he studied her face, as if searching for the right place to plant a kiss.

She wasn't worthy of his kisses and she tried to squirm away, more embarrassed than ever by the mess she'd brought into his world. Hiring her had forced his girlfriend out of the picture, and now that Lucy had proved secure boxes could be cracked, she'd put his reputation at risk.

He didn't let her get away, pulling her back to his hard body. "This wasn't a publicity stunt to embarrass me or the company?"

"No," she replied immediately.

"Good." His lips brushed her forehead. "Here's how this will go." He slid an arm around her waist and guided her to the couch. "We're going to sit here while you tell me everything." He removed his jacket and tossed it over the opposite chair. Sitting down, he situated her so she was sheltered by him, her hip pressed to his, his arm over her shoulder. With his free hand he traced the length of her fingers.

She couldn't remember the last time she'd felt so safe. Maybe with all the facts, Rush could find the way to save them all.

"Start at the beginning," he prompted gently.

She took another breath and let it all pour out.

"Kathrein didn't hire me because of my skills, he chose me because he needed someone who had a chance of infiltrating Gray Box."

"He wants my company?"

"No," she insisted. "He only wants the contents of Garmeaux's box."

"All right." Rush's fingertips traced lazy circles over her shoulder, much as he used to do when they snuggled in bed at the boathouse.

It was easier to admit all her failings when she could stare at his knee rather than look him in the eye. She told him everything from her first day as Kathrein's assistant right up to the day Gwen and Jackson were kidnapped, the old man's reasons, threats and everything else. The entire time, Rush's fingers kept circling her shoulder, stroking her hand. He didn't interrupt or ask any questions and when she finished, she thought her story sounded too bizarre to be believable.

"Show me the pictures and messages."

Her eyes gritty from crying and her body exhausted from days of unceasing tension, she felt as if she'd been hit by a truck as she retrieved her cell phone. She returned to find Rush standing at the window, legs wide, staring at the city spread out at his feet. With the stark contrast of his black tuxedo slacks and white shirt he reminded her of a pirate searching for new booty.

"Here."

He took her phone and scowled in concentration as he skimmed the text messages and pictures. "It was you trying to use that antiquated admin back door trick?"

She nodded. "Last night. The system locked me out after too many failed direct attempts on Garmeaux's box."

"Sam caught the attempts and accused me of planting bad seeds in young minds." He slid her phone into his pocket. "I should've known. You're the only woman who's ever listened to my stories."

"Maybe you should be more selective about your women." It surprised her that she could tease him in light of the circumstances.

He ignored the jab. "Sam didn't mention the IP address was the boathouse."

At least something had worked properly. "The admin back door wasn't the only thing I learned from our conversations."

His black eyebrows dipped low into another serious scowl. She wasn't sure she wanted to know what he was thinking now. "Are you going to let me go?"

"Hell, no."

Her heart plummeted. Gwen and Jackson were as good as dead if she couldn't convince him to let her take that information to Kathrein. "Rush, please. My sister's life—her son's life—is on the line."

"And they're your only family," he said. "I'm not the callous bastard you seem to take me for, Lucy."

"I've never thought that." She bit back the urge to protest further. She'd never found him callous, only singularly focused on business. A trait she would never ask him to change for the sake of her ego. "The callous bastard is Kathrein. I'm scared. No." She shook her head. "I'm terrified."

He pressed a finger to her lips to stop the brewing rant. Retreating, she curled into the end of the long couch and hugged her knees to her chest. Rush could think for days and it wouldn't change a thing. The first step in rescuing her sister and nephew was turning over the files.

"Sam noticed the problem and ghosted the box contents," Rush said, crouching in front of her.

"Oh, no." Lucy dropped her head to her knees and struggled not to give up. "If Kathrein suspects that, he'll come after you and the company." Every move she made exacerbated the problem.

"Telling you about a ghost box makes you only the third person in the world who knows it's possible," he said. "I think we're safe."

She heard him moving through the office, heard his fingers rapping on his keyboard and knew at the sound of his muttered curses he was reviewing the files on Kathrein.

"Lucy." His tone, more gruff than she'd ever heard

it, compelled her to look at him. "Even if you turn this over, he has to kill you."

"Haven't you been listening to me?"

"I'd hoped you were exaggerating, but your logic is sound."

"Gee, thanks." She rubbed her damp cheeks on her sleeve, grateful for the insult that put a little zip of heat into her bloodstream. Maybe the warmth was just the man himself. "No one ever has to know any of this happened—here, tonight."

"No way." He pushed a hand through his black hair.

"Then what?" She flung her arm toward his desk. "You just read it all, right?" At his nod, she barreled on. "Kathrein is old, but I can assure you he's no less ruthless than he was as a Nazi. The documents and pictures Garmeaux uncovered are convincing evidence that Kathrein assumed his dead cousin's identity to escape punishment for his war crimes. He's determined to see his grandson's political dreams come true. This entire mess is proof of how far he's willing to go. If he thinks I told you or involved the authorities, we're all dead."

"I'm not going to let that happen."

She stared into his vivid blue eyes and the resolute line of his jaw set her heart pounding. She wanted to believe his confidence over the stark facts. "Let me go, Rush. Let me go back to France and save Gwen and Jackson."

He crossed the office to sit beside her once more, taking her hand between both of his. "I have friends all over the world, Lucy. With a little time we can track down where he's holding your sister and the baby. Let me make some calls."

"No! You can't alert anyone or he'll kill them. He gave me a *week* and it's going by too fast. The man following me might already suspect I caved and told you. It has to be his way."

"We'll find a better option," he promised.

She shook her head, tears blurring her vision again. Why couldn't she stop crying? "I'm not taking you down with me. Destroy the ghost files," she pleaded. "Wipe out all record of Garmeaux. Forget I was here."

"I can't do that." His voice turned hard again. "I *won't* do that."

She opened her mouth to say more and he smothered the words with a kiss. What might have originated as a kiss of comfort ignited like a lit match, blazing across her senses. His lips moved over hers, hot and firm. She knew his mouth, the velvet stroke of his tongue, and recognized the urgency in his fingers. The familiar excitement sizzled along her nerves and danced through her bloodstream.

As if drawn by some invisible, magnetic force,

they moved together until she was under him, caged by his solid, sculpted chest and arms. She flexed her hips, grinding her eager body into his obvious arousal. He kissed her as if they'd never been apart and she responded in kind, releasing a year's worth of desire and yearning.

Scx and passion had never been their problem. Her body was pliant, already aching for the ultimate sensual satisfaction only Rush could give her.

"Lucy," he murmured as his lips skated down the column of her throat. "You don't know how I've missed you."

"I've missed you more than I wanted to admit was possible." She tugged at the studs of his tuxedo shirt until she could slide her hands inside. She moaned his name at the tantalizing combination of heat and strength under her palms.

His hands cupped her bottom, gripped hard as he drew her pelvis tight against his. He hiked up the fabric of her dress and his fingers followed the line of her panties across her backside. Oh, yes. She wanted to rewind the clock, to go back and relive some of their most sinfully mesmerizing nights.

She pushed at his chest until he sat up and she could straddle his hips, tugging his shirt free of his slacks. *He has the most glorious body*, she thought, running kisses across his chest. If this was her last week of life, she wouldn't let this last chance for plea-sure slip through her grasp.

"Lucy, wait." He brought her face back to his, kissed her lightly.

"I can't." She nuzzled that sensitive spot just under his jaw. If he stopped her now, she might start cry-ing again. "Please, Rush. I need you. Need you in-side me."

In the past those words would bring one of two reactions. Either more delicious, erotic foreplay or a swift and intense coupling that would leave her breathless.

"You've got me." His lips brushed hers again, feather soft. He gripped her waist and moved her to the side, pulling the skirt of her dress down over her legs. "You've got me, Lucy, but this isn't the time or place."

She laid a hand over his heart, buoyed that it beat as wildly as hers. She pulled back as far as his em-brace allowed, her dignity a lost cause. "Okay, I get it." She'd walked away from him in a desperate at-tempt at self-preservation, but her reasons were ir-relevant. Her decision, the way she'd executed it, had created a wedge between them, a distance she had to respect.

"How can you understand when I'm not sure I do?" He shook his head. "I'm going to take you home. You need rest. In the morning we'll come up with a plan that satisfies you, me and the bastard who sent you here."

"But—"

He gave her a squeeze. "Hush, sweetheart. You used to trust me."

Sweetheart. The phrase melted over her like warm chocolate as she met his gaze. Although she'd tried to relegate him to the back of her mind, tuck the memory of him behind a wall in her heart, she'd never really stopped trusting or loving this impossible man. "You won't make any calls tonight?"

"I won't if you won't," he replied.

"You have my phone," she pointed out.

He brought her hand to his lips, his breath warm on her skin in that pleasant instant. "I think I'll keep it. Just for tonight."

She thought that might be the best idea she'd heard in a long time.

Chapter Eight

Friday, December 18, 7:45 a.m.

Rush kept his promise to Lucy, but it proved to be one of the most challenging nights of his life. Just walking up to the door of the boathouse with her had made him break out in a cold sweat. He hadn't set foot inside the place since the day she'd left him. No, he'd hired a team to clean it up and maintain it for rental potential, although he couldn't bear the idea of strangers here, either.

Now he stood on the balcony off the living room, watching the fog roll across the span of the Golden Gate Bridge. Dressed for the day in jeans and a black button-down shirt with the Gray Box logo his house-keeper had sent from the condo, he sipped his coffee and waited for Lucy to wake up, as if the past year of personal hell hadn't happened. Only Lucy Gaines could bring him to his knees this way.

Last night in his office, his arms full of her, he

couldn't come up with the solutions she needed. All his attention had been diverted to far more primitive and immediate needs. Fearful that spending the night together in the boathouse would make matters worse, she'd apparently come to her senses and quickly disappeared into the guest suite. He'd woken in the master bedroom, alone and frustrated, with a few workable ideas.

Hopefully he'd be able to convince Lucy to give one of his ideas a try. He planned to start by researching every detail about the sneaky bastard holding her family hostage. Sam had ways of doing those searches without raising any suspicion. They needed confirmation of Garmeaux's findings. After that, there were friends he could call, friends with tactical skills, weapons expertise and successful track records with sensitive rescue missions.

Rush turned at the creak of a floorboard on the stairs. The once soothing sound put him on edge, uncertain how the night might have changed Lucy's perception of her situation. He walked inside and pulled the slider closed. Trying to greet her with a smile, he felt the gesture freeze on his face as she came around the corner.

She wore loose cotton boxers and a clingy tank top, her hair tousled from sleep. If not for the faint smudges of weariness under her eyes, he would have scooped her up and taken her back to bed until they were both sated. In the clear light of a new day, he didn't think she'd let him get away with that kind of distraction. It was likely best that they waited until after she was reunited with her sister and nephew.

He filled a mug with coffee, leaving room for cream, and set it on the counter for her. "Did you get any rest?"

"A little." Her mouth twisted side to side, lips pursed. "What about you?"

"A little," he echoed. He pulled the cream out of the refrigerator and passed it to her, along with a spoon and the sugar bowl.

She made a humming sound. "You remember."

He watched her over the rim of his mug while she slid onto the counter stool and doctored her coffee. She'd be shocked by how much he remembered. From every morning habit, to her favorite yoga studio and sushi bar downtown, to the sultry moans of pleasure when he was inside her.

Patience, he thought, keeping his ideas to himself while the caffeine did its work. He'd get her through this and then he'd win her back. He just had to resolve her trouble one step at a time. He'd sensed the fatalistic desperation pushing her last night in his office. He wanted her body, was pretty desperate himself, but not as a grand farewell to life. By some miracle he'd realized the timing would have backfired if he'd followed his body rather than his heart.

His *heart*? He nearly laughed. Lucy would freak out if she could read his mind right now. As close as they'd been, she accepted his theory that he only had a heart for his business and innovations. And she'd stuck by him, encouraging him every day, until the day she hadn't. It was a quirk unique to her that he hadn't been able to replicate with anyone else. No matter how he tried, how clear he was about expectations, women believed they could change him.

She walked around the counter to start rummaging for breakfast and he waited, rewarded when she burst into a happy dance at the sight of the bag of doughnuts from the kiosk across the street. "Oh, you got maple and bacon."

"Only the best."

She took his coffee cup out of his hands and gave him a fast, hard hug. "*You* are the best," she said emphatically as she stepped back. Pulling plates from the cabinet, she carried the bag to the table.

His chest ached at the normalcy of it as he brought the coffees along. He'd leave her phone in his pocket until she finished a doughnut. What he had to say would cast a pall over the morning and he wanted to put it off as long as possible.

"Any new messages from Kathrein on my phone?" she asked, licking frosting from her fingers.

His body reacted to the tempting sight of her lips closing around her fingertips with a predictable surge of arousal. The best defense against his physical needs was to give her the awkward news. He set the phone on the table. "Posturing, mostly," he assured her.

Her eyes went wide and her gaze darted from the device to his face and back again. "Mostly? Are there new pictures?"

"Not from Kathrein. I did take a few pictures of the man who might be his spy."

She blanched. "Do you think he's already...already hurt them?"

"No." Rush hated the fear and hurt in her big brown eyes. He reached out and covered her trembling hand. If he ever got his hands on Kathrein, he wouldn't be responsible for his actions. "He won't give up his leverage too soon."

"Leverage." She bit her lip and gazed out at the view of the bay. "I want to *kill* him for putting Gwen through this. She's been through enough already."

Rush stuffed the last bite of his doughnut into his mouth before he blurted out that he could make that happen. Better to keep *that* secret a bit longer. "I'm thinking there's quite a line ahead of you."

"What do you mean?"

He hesitated. Explaining could expose him. "I've looked into Kathrein before." The week he'd heard she'd been hired by the bastard. "Occasionally, our investment interests cross," he fibbed. "You're aware his lawyers and representatives have a reputation for being nasty?" She nodded and he continued, "My thought is that even without taking over his dead cousin's life, he became a recluse to make himself a smaller target."

"And yet there are plenty of people who benefit from the jobs he creates and the charities he funds."

"True." Rush pulled out another doughnut for each of them. "On the way to the office, I want us to be seen at the coffee shop two blocks up from the office."

"That's a popular place." She cupped her hands around her mug. "Why?"

"Because it *is* a popular place." He thought she'd already guessed his real reasons, but he spelled it out. "I want Kathrein to believe you're working me as a personal asset. It will also give us a chance to determine if the man I saw is, in fact, the spy."

She lifted her coffee mug and eyed him carefully. "Have you warned Trisha?"

"No need. My lawyers had a chat with her yesterday after her tantrum."

"Still playing hardball, I see."

She said it with a wry grin and he mirrored the expression. "Trisha's misguided behavior was effectively a breach of contract."

Lucy's brown eyes danced with amusement. "Is that the dating equivalent of a prenup? Do you require all your dates to sign a noncompete or nondisclosure agreement as well?"

He smiled broadly to hide his discomfort. "Nondisclosure is a must if they spend any time at Gray Box." Her comments struck too close to the bone. The return to the boathouse, the conversation, the very real threat to her were all piling up and making him want to hurry this along so he could capitalize on the moment. Only the awareness that, if he moved too soon, the consequences to her family as well as to his goals could be catastrophic kept him in check. "It is as calculating as it sounds," he confessed. "I like having someone with me at events but I refuse to let a woman think there's a chance for anything more than the terms strictly outlined. The contract protects everyone from unreasonable expectations."

"On the upside, you probably have your pick of spokesmodels for new products well into the next millennium."

He laughed, helpless against her honest, edgy wit. "There might be one or two I'd feel safe to approach for a launch down the road." He leaned in close. "At the moment, *you* are my sole priority."

"Rush."

Her breathy whisper slid under his defenses. Would it be so bad to take her to bed and make her forget the jerk in Chicago she'd used to replace him? "Don't tell me you're surprised."

"No. I always admired your focus." She barreled on before he could enjoy the compliment. "I didn't want to upend your life. You certainly don't owe me any heroic measures. Maybe we should use your publicity idea a little differently."

He braced his elbows on the table, eager to hear this. "I'm all ears."

"I'll take the information to Kathrein and trade it for Gwen and Jackson. He won't kill me if my name and face are in the spotlight, linked with yours."

"Are you forgetting he made the world believe Garmeaux died in an accident, Lucy?"

"Not at all." She grimaced. "You're different. Influential."

"It won't be enough," he stated. "I'm not going to let you martyr yourself."

"That isn't my intention." She pulled a knee to her chest and wrapped her arms around it. "So what's your next step after we play out the scene at the coffee shop?"

"We make some social noise, you send him an email that you're almost in, and then I'll make an announcement that you're a new key player at the Gray Box offices. Then, while the media is chewing on that, I'll apply all my effort, contacts and resources to locating your family."

"You can find them?"

"Yes," he said. With his friends it was absolutely possible. "It's the best plan," he pressed.

"It's an option with huge potential to backfire." Her gaze narrowed as she calculated the risks. "I'm running out of time."

Rush inhaled slowly. "Other than you, when have I failed at anything?"

Her lips parted on a surprised gasp and a jolt of desire shot through his system. If she remembered the effect she had on him, she'd learned to hide it well in the past year. Other than the hug, she hadn't even tried to touch him today. He cursed himself for stopping last night. The physical release could have benefitted them both and he might be able to focus on something other than his persistent state of arousal.

Her gaze lowered to his lips, then slid away to the view outside. She stood and paced to the window, leaning her forehead against the glass. The muted light painted her body and he had to resist the temptation to wrap her up in his arms.

"Have you worked up a program to find them?" she asked.

"In a manner of speaking," he replied. "If we're in agreement, I'll make a call and set things in motion."

She didn't move. "Who do you want to call?"

"I've made several interesting friends through Gray Box clients and contracts. Do you trust me, Lucy?"

"Yes."

Her immediate reply gave his ego a boost. Pushing back his chair, he gathered up the dishes and carried them to the kitchen sink. "I'll let you know more details on the way to the office."

"Okay." She turned, her arms wrapped around her midsection. "About last night…" Her voice trailed off, though her gaze remained steady.

"Can we table that discussion for now?" *Please*, he added silently. "Unless you think you'll have trouble being friendly and affectionate at the coffee shop."

Her smile was shy. "I won't have any trouble with that."

As she went upstairs to shower and dress, he hoped she meant it. However she'd come back into his life, he looked forward to reclaiming the closeness they'd once shared.

While he waited, Rush made several calls. Doubts pestered him as he turned over the various scenarios and outcomes and what they needed to do to rescue her family. He was the worst kind of hypocrite for being jealous and doubting her while resenting her for assuming the worst of his contract with Trisha. He'd told her the personal stuff had to wait, yet when she came back downstairs, he returned to the issue, inexplicably worried there was more she was hiding. "No one in your life will be upset seeing you with me?"

"Answer is still no." Her lips twisted to the side.

"Gwen, should she catch the news, will be thrilled. She always liked you."

He tried not to let the compliment go to his head. Call him a jerk for making her repeat it, but he felt better having a definitive answer. Lucy's only secret had been her kidnapped family. She never would have kissed him if she was involved with someone else. After all, she'd left Chicago to work in France.

"May I have my phone back?" she asked, slipping into black heels. She looped her computer bag over her shoulder and picked up her purse. "Rush?"

The woman mesmerized him and he couldn't stop staring, couldn't stop thinking of all the places on her body that he wanted to touch and kiss. She'd also chosen jeans today, but she turned casual to elegant with a snug white shirt topped with a colorful, long, open sweater. Silver drops at her ears were echoed in the silver necklace sparkling against the white fabric. And then there were those sexy black heels.

"Your phone." He held it out. "I may need to play with it later, depending on how the next few hours go."

They left the roadster in the garage and let the service do the driving. When the driver pulled to the curb at the coffee shop, Rush noticed his calls had been effective. The people from the right papers and blogs were there to see Lucy get out of the car with him. She played it perfectly, immediately reaching for his hand, leaning into his touch and smiling up at him.

He thought his face might crack under the pressure of holding back when he wanted so desperately to make the role they were playing real. She didn't know the shock and despair she'd created when she left him. No one did. Although he'd buried the surprising sense of loss and grief in work and made the expected social moves to keep up his image, he'd never given up on winning back Lucy. Psychologists and gossip rags would have a field day with that admission, he thought as he gazed into her warm brown eyes.

On the executive floor, Melva greeted them with such obvious delight he felt guilty. His office manager had always loved Lucy's effect on him, claiming she gave his life balance and stability. Of course, Melva often chided him for working harder than ten men just for the bragging rights.

He purposely left the privacy glass off as they drafted a press release about Lucy joining the Gray Box team. After another protest about the effect this would have on him and the company when she left, she agreed to let him send it.

"It won't be a problem," Rush assured her again, shoving his hands into his pockets. "Hell, with your reputation the stock is likely to go up." Here at the office he wanted to keep the affectionate displays to a minimum, if only so he didn't set himself up for her rejection. He was starting to think last night's kisses were the sum of stress, exhaustion and inhibitions reduced by darkness. "Now, let's get to the real problem. He gave you a week?"

"Yes. If I don't hand over the information by Monday, he'll kill them," she said, her voice tight. "Did you see the spy at the coffee shop?"

Rush nodded. "He tailed us from the boathouse. Kathrein will probably be in touch any minute."

Setting her phone on his desk as if it might explode, she pressed a hand to her stomach. "I can't stand this. My imagination is going crazy with how they're suffering."

Now he did turn on the privacy glass. "Sit or pace, but start talking. Tell me everything you know about Kathrein."

"I did that last night."

"I don't mean about the kidnapping or the reasons behind it. I want to know about the man. You were his personal assistant." He knew how quickly Lucy picked up facts and concepts. Her brain fascinated him as much as her beauty.

"Only for a month." She laced her fingers and rocked her hands back and forth while he stared her down. "Okay, okay." She sucked in a breath. "I know what you're getting at."

At his desk, he listened, making notes about Kathrein's living habits, ethics, the briberies she suspected, his staff and his most recent connections. Rush did this all while his mind and body indulged in a deep appreciation of her inherent grace as she paced the length of the windows.

When the company had moved into this building, he'd drafted dozens of emails with pictures, as excited as a kid at Christmas to share the success with her. He hadn't sent any of them and eventually had cleared them off his computer. An email reply, if she'd bothered to send one, wouldn't have satisfied him. He'd wanted her here, in person, so he could enjoy the thrill of her smile as she took in the expansive, inspiring views. He'd wanted to press her back against the glass and feel her legs lock around his hips as he drove himself into the tight heat of her body.

Before they'd made the leap from friends to lovers, he'd once overheard her protesting to a girlfriend that she wasn't his type. In an instant he was back at that moment, realizing how much better Lucy was than the glossy, empty women he typically dated to keep up appearances. He nearly laughed. It seemed Melva had a valid point.

Unique and beautiful, Lucy had enchanted him from the first question she'd asked during his guest lecture for her graduate program. He'd wanted to hire her on the spot but waited until they had more privacy over coffee after the class. She'd blown off him and his outrageous offer with her merry laughter.

That might have been the moment his obsession started, though he'd hidden his immediate needs. He eventually won her over with several casual dates, even working dinners, followed by extravagant surprises until finally landing in a bed during a weekend cruise on his yacht. There they'd discovered another mutual interest in creative, bold sexual play and passion.

God, she'd been a wonder, his ideal companion in every sense.

"Are you listening?" She'd stopped pacing and perched on the edge of one of the chairs in front of his desk, studying him with a narrowed gaze.

"Just thinking," he replied, quickly typing up the last thing he'd heard her say. "I'm going to forward this file to one of my contacts."

"I'm still not sure it's worth the risk."

He wiggled his eyebrows, trying to lighten her mood. "I know a few things about encrypting files."

"It's not that. If Kathrein could hack your system he wouldn't have sent me." She let out a frustrated oath. "He has a spy out there, proving he has a long reach and plenty of contacts, too. If you're suddenly taking meetings with tactical security experts, he'll assume I've told you what's going on. He's old, not stupid."

"I believe you. Now that my team isn't following you, looks like we've got an ID on the spy tailing you," Rush said as he skimmed an incoming email. He immediately returned his attention to the task of framing his more urgent request for help to locate and rescue Lucy's family. "We have several clients, from government agencies to private companies, who deal in security and tactical operations. Leaping to conclusions could wreck Kathrein's plan and though he might get suspicious, he'll have to bide his time. The man I've asked to help us could easily be explained as a client disconnected from our real problem. But don't worry, he won't come anywhere near us or the building." *Yet*.

"Back up a second."

Hearing temper simmering in her voice, he glanced up. "Yes?"

"*Your* team identified Kathrein's spy?"

"Just now, yes." He watched, wary as her cheeks and ears turned red. She rarely blushed unless she was angry. With a few strokes of the keyboard, he put the man's picture on a monitor mounted on the wall and added candid shots they'd collected over the past twenty-four hours. "Do you recognize him?"

She shook her head, her lips clamped shut.

"What makes this a problem?" he asked.

"You said you had me followed," she replied, her eyes hot.

"Would you believe it's standard procedure for new hires?"

"I would not." Lacing her fingers in her lap, her silence demanded his explanation.

"Well, it is. In certain cases." He came around the desk, ready to apply liberal amounts of charm to smooth over his careless handling of this detail. "I dug a little deeper. Kathrein has invested in two cyber security developers during the past six months," he said leaning against the desk. "Based on our current dilemma, now I understand why. Knowing you came to me directly from his employ, I had you followed. It wasn't personal," he fibbed. "Anyone coming from a similar situation would have been followed."

Her tension ebbed from her hands and mouth, but he could see she wasn't entirely convinced.

No matter how angry or offended she was, he would be grateful for the decision. His caution had resulted in an inadvertent and additional measure of protection for her that made the ensuing steps easier.

"YOU'VE CHANGED." LUCY held his gaze, her outrage over his invasion of her privacy fizzling. She should have expected it and, yes, in his place she would have done the same thing.

"Changed?" He stared at her and the blue depths of his gaze tempted her just as it always had. "No. Not on the things that matter most," he replied after a thoughtful pause. "You don't seem quite as angry."

"I have bigger problems." The way he'd been using

"us" and "we" and "our" made her heart melt, but at the end of the day this problem was between her and Kathrein. If she could spare Rush the grief and trouble, she would. "What can I do about the man following me?"

He shifted, obviously thinking it over. Folding his arms over his chest, he stretched out his long legs and crossed his ankles. Did he have to be so irresistibly sexy all the time? She hadn't been with anyone since Rush, and right now she regretted every missed opportunity. She'd dated in Chicago, mostly to appease her sister, but the enigmatic chemistry she shared with Rush had been missing. Wouldn't he crow with satisfaction if he knew?

It was too late for them. Rush wasn't the sort to forgive the way she'd left and he had no interest in addressing the needs of her heart. *Only my body*, she thought as another little spark of anticipation zipped through her.

From head to toe, her body was certain sex with Rush would be enough. Her greedy hormones urged her to reach out and take what she wanted from the man. Surely last night's sizzling kisses and embraces verified he'd be open to one last fling for the sake of closure. Her mouth went dry and her palms damp as her body warmed to the idea. Maybe, she thought, just maybe she would proposition Rush once Gwen and Jackson were safe. For closure.

He still hadn't answered her and she couldn't hide in his office forever. "Come on, Rush. What do you propose?" His eyes went wide and she immediately regretted her choice of words. Love, marriage and romance were foul words in his vocabulary. "Do we use the spy or ignore him?" she asked quickly. "Or should I call Kathrein right now to make the trade?"

"None of the above." Rush returned to his side of the desk. "I want you to go through the motions here at the office while I do some more research on this. We need to make it look like you're scrambling to meet the demands."

"Why doesn't he call?" She glared at her phone again. The constantly evolving knots in her stomach were making it difficult to breathe.

"We'll get through this," Rush said. "I'm fast and creative. We're only making it look like you're still working alone. I'm going to let Sam leak news about an attempted hack. That should convince Kathrein you're trying."

"All right." She stood up, determined to exemplify the courage and trust he was requesting. "You won't forget the deadline?"

"Not a chance."

"And you won't take any action without telling me *before* you do it?"

"Want it in writing?"

She held up her hands in surrender. "No, thank

you." He'd gone above and beyond when he could've reported her to the police. Rather than wrestling this out of her control and dropping her behind an army of guards while he solved her problem, he was keeping her close, keeping her involved. "I wish he'd confirm something about Gwen."

"Jackson looks content in every picture," Rush reminded her. "Can you believe he'd be that happy with only the care of Kathrein or his guards?"

When he put it in that context, a fraction of the tension lifted from her shoulders. "You're right."

"Almost always," he said with a cocky grin, until his eyes landed on his monitor and his thinking scowl returned. "I'll give you an hour at your desk, then we're taking a tour of the R & D floor."

"Yes, boss." She wondered what kind of software he had in Research and Development that could save her family. Her distraction didn't last long. While she was updating Rush's calendar and commitments, she received an email from the charitable foundation managed by Kathrein's daughters.

Reading it, Lucy swore under her breath. The innocuous message was an invitation to a holiday fundraiser on Tuesday, the day after her deadline. It had been addressed to the Gray Box email address HR had assigned to her yesterday.

Between the sexy, audacious man in the glass-walled office behind her and the nasty bastard playing grandpa with her nephew, she decided there were too many clever and resourceful billionaires in her life. When she fell in love again—assuming she could forget Rush long enough to give another man a chance—she would make sure to fall for a thoughtful, unassuming man with a net worth closer to the half-million mark.

Her light duties as an assistant left her mind free to wander down that diverting path. She and this currently featureless man of average means would get married and say "I love you" every day and leave the city for a typical suburban neighborhood in an excellent school district. They'd invest in a cozy house with a wide porch overlooking a bright green lawn all wrapped up with a white picket fence. There would be children and coffee-klatch friends and even a dog that enjoyed morning jogs with the anonymous man of her dreams.

Melva walked up and burst the bubble, presenting her with a paper plate of something that might have started as cereal before it had been turned into a bright green Christmas wreath the size of a bear claw. "Help me eat this," she said, breaking it in two.

Lucy eyed it cautiously. "You take the first bite."

"The green looks off-putting, I know, but it will be your new favorite," Melva said. "We can all be thankful Ken's wife only sends it in once a year."

"I think I need more information," Lucy said.

"Just hurry up and taste it," Melva insisted, pinching off another bite for herself. "You can't let me eat it all."

Lucy obeyed and the burst of sweetness on her tongue surprised her. "Holy cow. That's *good*."

"Exactly." Melva's smug expression made Lucy chuckle.

"You're crazy to share."

"A shared treat has fewer calories. Scientific fact. We can't all be as young and fit as you," Melva said. "You and Rush looked happy at the coffee shop this morning."

Lucy had to smile, to pretend their reunion was real. "It's nice to be back in town," she said, taking another bite to prevent any verbal slipups.

"You're just what he needs," Melva said with a wink before she walked back to her desk.

Lucy devoured the rest of the treat and licked the sticky bits and pieces from her fingers. She was mid-sigh, her lips clinging to the finger in her mouth, when Rush walked out of his office.

His gaze locked onto her mouth, his eyes full of an unmistakable lust. Going hot, her body leaned toward him, pure instinct and desire. Desperate, she swiveled the chair around and took a moment to pull herself together.

"Time for that tour. Bring the Gray Box tablet

along," he suggested. "Leave your phone here," he added under his breath.

She did as he asked and followed him to the elevators. He pressed the button for the express, and when the doors parted he encouraged her to enter first. She felt his eyes on her backside and quickly turned around to face him.

That made matters worse. The doors had barely closed when he pulled her in for a kiss. Nothing sweet or easy as he'd done at the coffee shop; this was a thorough possession, his tongue twining with hers in hot, velvet strokes. She gripped his sleeve with her free hand to keep her balance.

He made a little humming sound in his throat. "You taste like Christmas."

"You can't kiss me here." She protested, trying to establish an appropriate distance though it was far too late.

His fingers flexed on her hips and he kissed her again. "Seems like I can." The car stopped and he reached over and smacked at the panel. His hands slid under her sweater, up her spine, setting her nerves on fire through her shirt. "No cameras in here. Don't worry."

A year ago that might have made her feel better. Right now she could only imagine the other women he'd kissed in here since the building had opened. The thought that she was bookending his flings turned her voice sharp. "Are we going to R & D at all or was it a ploy to get me in here for an elevator quickie?"

He stepped back, looking a little hurt. "Tempting as you make that sound, we are down here for a reason."

"I'm sorry," she began.

"No." He cut her off. "I should apologize." He hooked his thumbs in his back pockets with a heavy sigh. "Kissing you last night opened the floodgates for me. I don't want to stop."

She bit back the admission that would only urge him on, searching for a way to be honest without giving him the wrong idea. "I understand," she said. It sounded lame to her ears. "Better if I could kiss you without the distraction of your reputation and Kathrein's leverage hanging over my head." That was a far more honest and complete answer.

He grinned. "You're worried about my reputation?"

She rolled her eyes at him. "Yes. You have a company with global interests to protect. A different woman every week can make investors worry about your stability."

"Oh, bull. You don't believe that garbage any more than I do. Gray Box is the best program of its kind. My investors appreciate the returns and our clients appreciate the security we offer. Why are you really pushing me away?"

She couldn't admit she was trying *again* to mitigate the risk to her heart. Steamy kisses and blazing sexual chemistry hadn't been enough for her a year ago. By his own admission, the romantic happy-ever-after didn't suit Rush. She didn't want him to resent her for having feelings he couldn't reciprocate.

"Kathrein will surely retaliate if he discovers you've helped me," she said, seizing on the most logical argument. "You've worked hard, Rush. I don't want to put all of your effort and success in jeopardy."

"I can deal with any corporate attack," he said. "What else?"

"We're at the office." She clutched the tablet to her chest like a shield. "You said we'd table talking about us. Why do you keep bringing it up?"

"Now is later enough for me," he said with a shrug. "What did last night mean to you?"

To her chagrin, she felt a wave of tears brimming. If there had been an escape hatch, she would have leaped through it rather than face him at this low point in her life. "You listened with compassion." She could stick with the truth and still protect herself. "Rather than turn me over to the authorities, you offered to help me. I appreciate that more than words can say." His gaze narrowed and a chill slid down her spine, bumping along over each vertebra.

"You ripped open my shirt and crawled all over me as a show of appreciation?"

"You started that part," she snapped. Her jaw was cramping, her teeth were clenched so tightly. "Stop making it bigger, more important than the flash of lust between old lovers." Desperate for a way out of this elevator as well as the unbearable conversation, she reached for the control panel and pushed the Open Door button, but the doors didn't budge. "Come on, Rush. Nothing really happened."

"Huh. I'm not feeling much appreciation for my extraordinary restraint and courtesy," he said.

"Why are you picking a fight?"

"I want to know where the boundaries are."

The man made her want to scream. She calmed herself with a quick visual of pounding some sense into his thick skull. "It's not as if we ever had many of those."

His grin flashed across his face and disappeared so quickly she thought she imagined it. "If it wasn't solely a matter of appreciation, what prompted you to rip open my shirt?"

"Stop saying that!" She clapped a hand over her mouth at the outburst. "You're impossible!"

"Is that why you walked out on us?"

She'd walked out because she needed him too much and he never thought twice about leaving her stranded, consistently less valuable than his growing business. "This is not the time or place," she said, using his words from last night.

"I'm not opening the doors until you give me an answer."

"To which question?"

He shrugged. "Lady's choice."

"Fine. You win." Her free hand fisted at her side. "Last night I wanted to take every ounce of comfort any way I could get it," she said, keeping her voice low. "Last night I wanted to forget the terrible moments of recent days and sink into the memories of how good we were together." His chest swelled with pride at her words. "Last night I was grateful for your common sense as well as your kindness and thoughtfulness. You were a perfect gentleman. But right this second?"

"Yes?" he urged.

"I'm working to remember that you're going above and beyond to help me. Right this second, if I had a better option to save my family, I'd give in to the urge and give you a kick rather than let you steal another kiss."

"You're mad at me?"

Her shoulders sagged. "That sums it up, yes."

"Then we're even."

"Pardon?"

He caught her chin and held her gently, forcing her to meet his gaze. "Here are a few answers to questions I wish you would ask me. I was furious when you moved to Chicago. Livid when you replaced me with another man. I promised myself if you ever stepped foot in San Francisco again, I'd find a way to infuriate you in kind."

"Payback?" When he nodded she barely kept from giving him that kick. His tirade, his anger over something personal was so out of character she could hardly process the words. She opened her mouth to admit she'd lied about the new boyfriend and caught herself in the nick of time. She couldn't leave herself that vulnerable. "You do know how obnoxious that sounds?"

"Yes." His smile of pure satisfaction made her pulse skip. "I don't plan to stop, although I'm done being mad about it." His lips feathered across hers once more and then he reached for the elevator panel.

She caught his arm, stalling him. "You realize I was mad at you when I moved to Chicago? You being mad at me made us even last year."

"How could I have known?" He tugged free of her grasp and pressed the button to release the doors. "You didn't stick around long enough for us to kiss and make up."

The doors parted to reveal a small crowd of people who scrambled back in a comic tangle, pretending they hadn't been eavesdropping on the private conversation.

Finally his behavior and the bizarre argument made more sense to Lucy. Like the coffee shop earlier, he'd staged a scene that would underscore her role here, in case Kathrein's spy managed to get someone inside Gray Box to talk.

In spite of the sudden, lonely ache in her chest and the sting of tears behind her eyes, she had to give him points for the performance.

Chapter Nine

While his blood pounded from the combination of impossible arousal and heated argument, Rush introduced Lucy to everyone and gave her an extensive tour of the R & D floor. He ignored the smirks and speculative glances along the way. He should've thought about the potential gossip, especially on the heels of Trisha's tantrum, and kept himself in check.

No one would dwell on it long. Most of his employees assumed the worst about his social life anyway. "Spoiled billionaire" and "incorrigible player" had become more common descriptors for him than the previous references to his brilliant ideas and business savvy. He endured it by imagining the utter shock on their faces if they knew how completely his relationship with Lucy had altered him.

She made him think and feel on a completely different level. Though it was more than lust, he knew it wasn't love. He needed her and he valued her. He'd thought those feelings had been mutual.

Watching her, guilt nagged at him for picking a fight. When Lucy was close, conflicting priorities went to war inside him. He wanted to confide his latest concepts and keep her at arm's length. He wanted to charge into battle beside her and whisk her off to an island where Kathrein would never find her. He wanted to show her the facets of his personality only being with her had revealed.

More shocking was the urge to admit he hadn't slept with anyone since she'd walked away, but the confession battered against his pride every time he thought about her replacing him. The public displays of affection with his various dates had been nothing but smoke and mirrors. Now that she was here, the self-inflicted abstinence was starting to take a toll. The next time a kiss turned that hot, he wouldn't let either of them off the hook. That was one good reason to start applying some of his notorious self-control.

She made notes as they moved along and he explained the potential of several projects. Her astute questions reinforced his opinion that they were a smart match in any industry. Her mind was as gorgeous as the rest of her.

When they reached the far end of the lab, he aimed a hard look at the closest team and the trio quickly moved out of earshot.

"I had more questions," she said.

"So ask. I'll give you the answers." He picked up

a plastic ring, examining the piece that made up part of a drone propeller so he wouldn't be mesmerized by her eyes.

"Uh-huh," she murmured. "I had no idea you were working on so many hardware applications."

"I don't intend to bring all of these ideas to the general market. We're integrating cutting-edge software for a few specific applications."

"For a few contracted clients, you mean."

"Yes." He ran his finger over the seamless plastic repeatedly. If he looked at her, he'd be hard-pressed to maintain that self-control he'd just promised to apply. "We might take a few of these out for a field test in a day or two," he added. They had only three full days left to find her family.

He took her quiet gasp for understanding. Several of the cameras, drones and surveillance programs being developed down here could help them find and capture Kathrein without Lucy caving in to his demands. It would never be official and he'd never be able to brag about it, but if any of these devices worked, the right people would be more confident and inclined to sign his development teams for additional projects.

"Which item is closest to completion?"

He met her gaze. "For general market?"

"Sure." She held her stylus over the tablet, ready to make notes.

"The drone cameras have the greatest consumer potential. They're completely operational now. We're just tweaking the software to make it more user-friendly and we're beefing up the optics quality to meet expectations."

"That's exciting."

She sounded more pensive than excited. "And?" he prompted.

"You still face the issues of who can fly drones and where," she said. "The market seems limited."

"Don't you believe a small market is worth my time and attention?" He walked around the end of the worktable, hoping she understood they were discussing far more than his position leading the field of cutting-edge technology.

What he focused on, he brought to life. He didn't give up on technology or people.

He scowled at the plastic ring and carefully set it down. He'd never given up on having her in his life again. Telling himself he was giving her space, honoring her wishes, he'd never moved on with someone new. He refused to squander this chance to win her back, no matter what stood in his way.

An enormous pressure weighed on his shoulders. There was far more at stake than his happiness or his ability to make Lucy happy. Even with his skills and connections, there were no guarantees. Kathrein held the lives of her family in his hands. An overwhelming desperation washed over Rush. He would do anything to reunite Lucy with her family and spare her any more grief and loss. That mattered above all else. She evaded him, keeping the worktable between them. "How would you like me to proceed as your assistant? I can draft press releases or contact trade magazines about interviews or events."

"We're not at that stage yet, although the teams are eager for that step."

"So how does the stunt in the elevator and this little tour affect a certain French hostage taker?"

"He's not French."

"Not the point." She rolled her eyes. "Do you think someone down here is working for Kathrein?"

"Absolutely not. We're keeping up appearances. I wanted you to see I have the tools to assist the particular situation. If you'll trust me." He supposed if he wanted her trust he should stop irritating her at every turn.

"Got it." Her gaze slid toward the other end of the room and then she peered at him from under her thick, dark lashes. "Thank you." She cleared her throat. "You have two appointments this afternoon and the first is scheduled in fifteen minutes."

They returned to the executive floor in silence, each of them lost in thought. Rush valued the quiet as much as the fact that his first appointment was early.

If Lucy recognized Parker Lawton's name as he

ushered his friend into his office, she didn't show it. Calling in this favor was a big risk. Despite what he'd told her, if the man Kathrein sent to keep an eye on Lucy caught wind of this, Rush might have blown the element of surprise.

Kathrein had given Lucy an impossibly tight time-line to crack the strongest cyber security company in the world. While Rush assumed it was to bring the matter to an end swiftly, he wanted to be sure they weren't missing a critical piece of the puzzle.

Lawton, formerly with military intelligence, now consulted and conducted investigations for private clients, like Rush. He knew how to track down real-world intel almost as fast as Sam could unravel a trail online.

Flipping the switch for the privacy glass, Rush asked, "What did you find?"

"Not as much as I could get with even one more day," Lawton replied. "Paris officials did rule the journalist Garmeaux's death an accident, but you were right to be suspicious." He held up a hand to waylay Rush's question. "I don't have anything conclusive. His boss said he was on the story of a lifetime, but he hadn't turned anything in. All the normal substance screens were clear but the witness reports don't add up and the bike disappeared from police custody."

"Not good." Rush resisted the urge to get up and pace.

"Nope," Lawton agreed. "As for the other issue, Dieter Kathrein is definitely a paranoid recluse. The public persona is managed by his daughters and his grandson who is poised to make a big political splash."

"What about his real estate? Did you find him?"

Lawton slid a report across the desk. "This is every property I could tie to him in Europe." He sat back. "That email attachment you sent me is pretty inflammatory."

Rush had only sent Lawton two pages of documentation connecting Kathrein to the Nazi regime. "Is it true?" A silly question considering the bastard was holding Lucy's family hostage to keep a lid on the information.

Lawton nodded. "While I'd appreciate more time to verify any loose ends and conduct my own interviews, my answer is yes, Kathrein assumed his dead cousin's identity. On top of that, my contacts were able to verify Garmeaux had been reaching out for interviews and diving deep into Kathrein's past. If he brought this report to your attention, be confident he was exercising due diligence, not throwing out wild accusations."

Rush let out a low whistle. "If this gets out, the consequences will destroy his grandson's political dreams. There's no way to spin a family fortune built on lies and war crimes."

"It's unfortunate," Lawton said. "The grandson could be an asset in French government. He's smart as a whip and well-respected. I'm currently checking to see if he shares his grandfather's old ideals, or if he is as ignorant of the truth as the rest of the world seems to be. No charge for that, it's my own curiosity."

"Any idea if the journalist had a safety valve on the story in case he died?"

"If he did, it fell through. The man's been dead for weeks and so far there's not so much as a whisper anywhere in Europe about this story."

Meaning Kathrein had every reason to believe controlling the content of the Gray Box would clear up everything. "All right."

Lawton bounced his fist on his knee. "My guess is the hard evidence connecting Dieter Kathrein to the Nazis by his real name is still buried in war tribunal records. Using the French Kathrein family tree I did a fast track through the German branch and called in a favor, as well." He cleared his throat. "To be fair, there were several men on that side of the family who joined the Nazi party. In particular, a young officer never returned from his assignment in Mauthausen and was presumed killed by Allied forces when the Austrian extermination camp was liberated. It would have taken time, but it's entirely possible for a young man to trek through the mountains and escape into France. If you want him prosecuted, I can track down his service record."

Rush scrubbed at his jaw, two days' worth of stubble rough against his fingers. "Not today, but I definitely intend to see him prosecuted." There was no statute of limitations on the crimes Kathrein committed.

Lucy would be furious when he explained Lawton's visit. He respected her concern about more people becoming targets, but asking the right questions was the only way to understand their enemy. They needed solid intel before they attempted a rescue. As she'd said last night, Kathrein would believe the only way to guarantee his family continuing generations of peace would be to eliminate Lucy. Not a stretch considering Kathrein's cruel and merciless past and present. Rush would not allow the old man's plots to end in tragedy for any of them.

"Thanks for your time and discretion," Rush said, coming around the desk to shake Lawton's hand.

His friend hesitated on his way to the door. "Can I ask how you came across this?"

"Only if I don't have to answer," Rush replied.

"I know you and your assistant, Grayson. She worked for Kathrein. Speaking hypothetically, if you take action on this, it won't be long before someone tags her as your source."

"It wouldn't be true," Rush stated.

"We both know truth doesn't always prevail."

He wasn't worried about Lucy's standing in the media. His priority was keeping her and her family alive. "We're also both well aware that having more money than God and dozens of lawyers on retainer can do a great deal to scrub away any mud."

"Billionaire against billionaire." Lawton cocked one eyebrow. "The press would make that interesting."

"Hypothetically speaking, what you're suggesting won't make the news," Rush replied. "When I move on Kathrein, it won't be public."

Lawton rocked back on his heels. "Good. My speedy verification isn't enough to take those documents public. I'd like more time."

Time was the only commodity Rush couldn't afford. Impatience snapped like a whip across his shoulders. "It's a delicate negotiation," he added, with a calm he didn't feel. "Things go better when I know the nature of the person calling the shots."

"Better you than me." Lawton rolled his shoulders. "I feel nasty just from the research. Why aren't you reporting him and walking away?" Lawton stared him down. "What are you and Lucy really up to?"

Rush swore. Lawton always saw too much. "I didn't give you all of it," he admitted. "The dead journalist stumbled on this story when he discovered a money trail from a Kathrein charity to a defense fund for a recently found war criminal, Alfred Portner. He went looking for an explanation."

"Holy crap."

Rush could see the wheels turning as Lawton made connections. "That's putting it mildly, my friend."

"You need more than a PI if you want to pin him for murder."

"Yes, I will, and soon." He'd intended to raise the topic with Lawton after he and Sam narrowed down a location, but a head start would only help. "What are you prepared to offer?"

"Anything you need."

"Sit down." Rush filled him in on the kidnapping and together he and Lawton reviewed the information he'd gathered on the European estates and assets. When they had a basic plan in place, Lawton agreed to go down and spend time with Sam.

Rush ushered Lawton past Lucy's desk and straight to the elevators. "Thanks for your time," he said.

"Be careful, Rush," Lawton said under his breath as he stepped into the elevator.

"You, too." He clapped his old friend on the shoulder. If everything went well, they'd see each other soon.

Returning to his office, he paused at Lucy's desk. "Cancel the next meeting. We need to talk."

"All right." She took care of it and stood, gracing him with a cool, professional smile. "I'm all yours."

With those three words, he was immediately aroused. Closing his office door behind them, he switched on the privacy glass and pulled her into his arms for a deep, lingering kiss.

"Stop it." She made a small effort to pull away. "We're at the office."

"I'm aware." He stepped back and tucked his hands into his pockets. "Thank you for coming to me, for trusting me." His pulse raced at the looming danger, though she was right here, safe and whole. He believed her sister and nephew were still alive and yet his entire being wanted to give in to panic.

"I came to your *company* to break into your system."

Semantics. "And you did." That she'd succeeded made him far happier than it should. "We knew about the breach, but you actually did it."

She gawked at him. "What is *wrong* with you?"

"Nothing." He moved toward his desk, drawing the file on Kathrein's properties out of her reach. "Never mind. That meeting just made me think."

"Uh-huh." She folded her arms over her chest and stared him down. "That was Parker Lawton."

"You remember him?"

"I remember you're good friends. I remember how

he'd dig up the background on people you planned to deal with."

He sank into his chair. "That still holds." She was perfect for him. He should have taken better care with her the first time around. If there was any constancy in his life, it was his refusal to repeat his mistakes. Once this crisis was resolved, he would convince her they belonged together. Not for a night or a few more weeks, but for a lifetime. She might not realize it, but they were the ideal team. Love had nothing to do with it, he reminded himself.

She planted her hands on her hips and glared at him. "You asked him to investigate Kathrein."

He swallowed, sensing this was the defining moment. This was the time to start a new habit of complete honesty with the only woman he'd ever trusted with his true self. Twenty, hell, fifty years from now he'd look back and realize this was the moment his life changed. "I did."

"Rush!" Fiery temper blazed in her eyes. "What if—"

"Hear me out."

"Then talk fast. When did you even reach out to him?"

"I checked his availability before you woke up this morning."

"So much for teamwork," she said with a sexy little snarl.

"I called him before we discussed teamwork." He sobered. "Are you going to listen?"

She mimed locking her lips and tossing away the key.

"Great. It bothered me that Kathrein chose this particular week to send you on mission impossible."

"As you pointed out, not so impossible."

"Noted," he agreed with a wink. "Still, why now? So far, his money has kept his past buried." He held up a finger when she started to answer him. "It's more than the grandson's political bid. Look, I asked Lawton to verify two pages of documentation I claimed I'd received on Kathrein. I didn't tell him where it came from."

"He recognized me and assumed."

"You know, he worried you'd get blamed if I released any of the nasty skeletons in Kathrein's closet."

"How thoughtful."

"Just logic," Rush corrected. He'd prefer it if she didn't aim warm compliments at other men when she'd been kissing him as recently as two minutes ago. "Sit down, Lucy." He waited for her to take the nearest chair. "You saw the files. Kathrein gave money to support the defense of one of his old Nazi buddies. Garmeaux followed the money. While there's no real proof, we agree with you that Kathrein silenced him."

She pressed her fingers to her lips. "What if the

spy tells Kathrein a man with Parker's history met with you today?"

"Lawton can take care of himself," Rush said. "This company has enough things going on locally and globally that Kathrein can't be sure I had him here to help you."

Her gaze dropped to her lap. "I hope you're right."

"I am." He was betting everything on his being right. Despite the disturbing news about the timing and increasing threat to Lucy, he would beat Kathrein at his own game.

She sat back farther in the chair and crossed her legs at the knee. "What other steps have you taken in your role as team captain?"

He eyed her cautiously. "Are you mad at me again?"

"No," she said, resigned. "But I'm not happy. You promised me we'd handle this together."

"We are. We will. Did you expect my part to be sitting back and holding your hand while he tormented you? Should I just watch quietly from the corner while you throw yourself on his nonexistent mercy?"

"STOP IT. NEITHER of us can afford to be mad. It gives him the advantage." Lucy knew her reactions were unreasonable. Rush cared for her. Whether as an old friend or as a new friend with benefits, the result was the same. "I'm overwhelmed. Yes, I need to *stay* in the loop, but it all feels insurmountable. He could have my family stashed anywhere." She didn't give voice to her worst fear—that he'd staged the pictures and already disposed of Gwen and Jackson. Her heart twisted painfully.

Rush looked to the ceiling and tapped his fingertips lightly on the desktop. His hands, so strong, so capable of creating blinding pleasure, had always captivated her.

"Everything I have is yours, Lucy. Every contact and favor owed me, every dollar and resource will be allocated to save all three of you from Kathrein. He'll put up a fight. It's what survivors do."

"Please…" Her voice trailed off as her heart fluttered in her chest. Words failed her that he would make such a complete pledge. "Enough." She swiped a hand through the air as if the grim images of the looming fight could be erased. "Just tell me how we can beat him. There are only three days left," she finished, though neither of them needed the reminder.

"Background always helps me, right?" It was a rhetorical question. "I've been thinking Kathrein made a mistake taking hostages. For seventy years he's escaped discovery, hiding behind his fortune and support network. His habit of arrogance will be our advantage."

"I hadn't thought of it that way," she mused. "In France, everyone is loyal to him."

"Everyone he let you meet, anyway."

"Oh, I'm an idiot." She twisted her hands in her lap. "Yes, the man's been a recluse because he's afraid to be identified. During my short tenure, the minimal staff wasn't simply about his preferences, but about who he trusted to keep his deepest secrets."

Rush nodded, encouraging her as she reviewed her time with Kathrein and his staff through this new lens. "I don't think he's taken your family out of France." He reached for a file folder. "We'll pack up some gear from R & D and take my plane. Once we pinpoint where he's holding your family," he added, "we can devise a rescue."

"That sounds fabulous, until you remember he'll kill Gwen and Jackson if he discovers I roped you into helping me."

"Roped me into it?" Rush stopped himself, staring at her with something that might have been pain in another man's eyes. "We'll clear that up later. As for Kathrein, you can count on me." He tapped his chest, showing a great deal of his own brand of arrogance. "I've been a master of diversion and illusion since my first hack as a kid."

She trusted him with puzzles and solutions. She trusted his mysterious resources—having seen an aging billionaire, she could only imagine the protection a man with Rush's modern, technical savvy would have in place. Oh, she trusted him, with everything…except her heart.

Emotions were the one life lesson Rush hadn't bothered learning. He knew how to get along, when to be tough, how to play fair or fight dirty, and he could woo women and clients with almost equal expertise. She knew enough about his childhood to understand his reluctance to let people get close enough to hurt him. Compound that with the fact that in order to maintain his place as a leader in the industry he had to shelter his feelings the way his company protected data.

She'd often wondered if he realized how well he cared for the people who depended on him. Not only Gray Box clients with the product, but the employees who loved working for him. Melva had been the first to give Rush and Sam legitimacy as they turned an idea into a thriving enterprise.

As the king of data and analysis, he had to know how rare lasting partnerships were. In study after study during her grad school days, partners split over big and small disputes. Rush and Sam, both ambitious geniuses, continued to beat the odds.

"Lucy?"

She was startled to discover he'd pulled a chair close to hers and was holding her hand between his larger palms. "My mind wandered."

"I noticed. What's the last thing you heard?"

She squinted, thinking. "You're a master of diversion."

He grinned with approval and gave her fingers a

squeeze. "Well, while you were lost in thought, Sam sent a text message. He's on his way up with news."

"Great." What a relief she hadn't missed the entire rescue plan while her mind catalogued Rush's admirable qualities. Why did she love the one man who didn't ever want to be in anything more than lust?

He'd told her more than once that her acceptance of his priorities was as much a turn-on as her adventurous sensual curiosity. She'd been careful not to expect or hope for him to change, just as she'd been very aware of the generous spirit he hid behind layers and layers of personal defenses and alternate vocabulary. He was capable of loving; his actions proved it repeatedly though he'd kick her to the curb if she phrased it that way.

And she'd fallen in love with him anyway. She still loved him, despite his autocratic tendencies and his conviction that love wasn't a viable option for his life. Why? Probably those bone-melting kisses.

He'd shown tremendous affection and care when they were dating. If last night was any indicator, the chemistry between them remained, as did the mutual respect. Maybe closure sex wasn't a good idea, after all.

He got up and crossed to a cabinet on the far wall that turned out to hold a small refrigerator. He returned with a bottle of water. "Here, drink up."

She did as he asked, the cold liquid clearing the

last of the cobwebs from her mind as Sam walked in. Of course Sam had something. The man could find a needle in any remote haystack of the internet without disturbing the haystack.

Sam gave her a warm, rocking hug and then held her at arm's length and studied her with concern from behind his black-framed glasses. "How are you holding up?"

She glanced past Sam to Rush. "It's good to have friends helping me." Helping her family. "Thank you." She sidestepped, forcing her lips into a smile. "Rush said you have news."

"I've found all kinds of dirt on the wealthiest recluse in France." Using the tablet in his hand, he entered a command and a panel slid back, revealing the bank of monitors on the far wall. "Did you have any idea you were working for such a tough old bastard?" he asked while pictures and data filled the screens.

"I knew the old part," Lucy said. "Tough was implied based on his business accomplishments and holdings. As for bastard, he was kind to me. At first."

Sam gave a dismissive grunt, a trait she remembered from the days when he and Rush would tackle one idea from two different angles.

"I worked the timeline backward from your arrival. Your sister and nephew must still be in France.

In fact, I don't think they can be far from the estate near Chantilly."

She stepped closer, examining the list of properties owned by the extended Kathrein family. There were estates scattered around Europe. "He only had a few hours," she murmured. "With planes and helicopters, that doesn't narrow it down much."

"This will." Sam changed the displays to a sky view of France. Small squares of various colors had been added to mark Kathrein's personal properties. There was a red square around the estate where she'd worked and lived, and another farther east near Strasbourg. Everything else had a different color.

"This winery." Sam zoomed in on the second red square. "It's one of the oldest properties in the deck. Production ended decades ago. When the Kathrein girls were young, the family vacationed there regularly. The views must be amazing," he said on a wistful sigh.

"Sam," Rush interjected.

"Right." Sam cleared his throat. "The family last visited more than five years ago and yet power was turned on last week. The family, aside from Mr. Recluse, of course, has been accounted for, going about their business in other parts of the country."

Pictures of Kathrein's daughters and their families filled the far third of the display.

"What about homes in urban areas he might be using?" Rush asked.

"Doubtful," Lucy said. "He really despises crowded areas."

"Sure that's not an act?" Rush asked. "He's lived another man's life all this time."

"Necessity or nature, at this point it hardly matters," Lucy said. "If his goal is to protect his grandson's reputation and plans, he's not going to take a chance of being caught with hostages in an urban area."

"I agree." Rush folded his arms over his chest while he reviewed the pictures. "We can run a cursory check on the city properties," he added. "But you and I will head for the winery." He reached for his cell phone.

Lucy turned to him. "We're going now?"

He nodded to her while he gave instructions to whomever was on the other end of the call, presumably someone at an airfield.

She bit her lip and it felt like an eternity before Rush was off the phone. "When he learns I've left with you," she warned, "that you're helping me, he'll ruin you. After he kills them." She couldn't live with that on her conscience—assuming she lived at all. Her stomach threatened to rebel again.

"Take it easy, Lucy. I can cover for you here," Sam said. "We have ways to make it look like you're both still working on this problem right here in the city."

She didn't bother asking how. Sam and Rush had amazing computer skills. She turned to Rush. "What about the spy he has tailing me?"

"The private cars and a lookalike team should keep him busy."

She pressed her fingers to her mouth, wanting to believe. He wandered around like a normal guy most of the time and then called in his extensive resources and connections when the situation justified it. "And how are the two of us going to save my sister and her son? He has armed guards and I'm certainly not current on combat rescue training." She'd wait until she and Rush were alone to make her argument that if they were wrong and Kathrein was using the winery as a decoy, storming the place would tip him off.

She could already hear him telling her to think positively and start envisioning scenarios with better endings.

"Do your part as planned," Rush said to Sam, with a tip of his chin to Lucy. "I'll handle this."

Lucy waited until Sam was safely on his way back downstairs. "Now I'm a 'this' to be handled."

"Yes," he answered without the first sign of remorse. "Can't you see how much I want to handle you?"

"Not funny." His words sent some enticing scenarios through her mind, all with very satisfying endings.

"A man can dream," he quipped. "Lucy, I'll be

honest, I'd rather you stayed out of harm's way and let my friends handle the rescue."

"Are *you* staying behind?"

"No. Someone who knows the tech gear we have in mind has to be on site."

She really should ask what that meant. Standing there, his expression so earnest, she almost felt guilty for walking away from him a year ago. If she'd stayed in San Francisco, Kathrein would never have been able to use her this way. But if she'd stayed with Rush she would have settled for loving a man who didn't want to love her back. It wouldn't have been awful, but it wouldn't have been right. "You found someone to double for me, too?"

"Yes." He tucked his hands into his pockets, watching her. "I know you and your mannerisms. I know you'd rather be right there with me rather than somewhere safe, wringing your hands and worrying."

The words sent a shiver down her spine and her heart did a silly flop in her chest. "Did you pack for me, too?"

He did a double take and then he laughed. "No. I hired that done. To an outsider, it looks like I moved back into the boathouse with you. In all the commotion, a packed suitcase wound up in the car that will soon take us to the airport."

"You didn't give me much to do besides hold a thumb drive we won't deliver."

"On the contrary." He held out his hand. "You can hold on to me. We wouldn't have made it this far without your insight and composure."

His comments surprised her. "Then I guess I'll be grateful you've thought of everything."

"Smart lady." He smoothed a stray lock of hair behind her ear.

Lucy managed not to shiver at the touch. While he called for the car, she wallowed in the compliment that chased away the dread that had been twisting in her gut since Sam's presentation.

After today, they only had two days to either cooperate or outwit Kathrein. She felt a ray of hope that, with Rush's resources and gear, they all might survive the coming finale.

Chapter Ten

Rush kept a close eye on Lucy as they left the office under cover and slipped into the backseat of a generic sedan with heavily tinted windows. She'd only said a few words since he'd set the plan in motion. The two of them would arrive first in France and would oversee the reconnaissance while Lawton pulled together a rescue squad.

Although Rush wanted to draw Lucy into conversation, he couldn't bring himself to push her too hard. Knowing her as he did, he gave her time to process the swell of information and the space to mentally prepare for the flight.

She wouldn't falter. Once Lucy made up her mind she didn't waste time second-guessing. It was one of her finest traits, even though it had worked against him a year ago. He'd been startled and confused when she'd walked out. After the shock had worn off, the anger and hurt had settled in and stayed. It had taken him months to look past her hurried departure and realize, being Lucy, she would have given the decision plenty of thought.

He wondered if she wished they could talk about it as much as he did. Their past wasn't the right discussion when she was so obviously frantic about her sister and nephew. Neither was it the right time to discuss their future, though he intended to clear the air on both topics soon.

She sat on the couch across from him in his jet, her face turned slightly to the window, but he knew she didn't see anything. Heading east at this late hour at high altitude, there wasn't much to see except clouds and the occasional patch of the Atlantic Ocean far below them. They had a few hours left and he'd encouraged her to lie down in the bedroom, but she'd been too restless.

In the silence, Rush's mind churned through possibilities as updates came in from Sam and Lawton. During the refuel in New York, Lucy had reminded him that Kathrein maintained the loyalty of plenty of police and officials. It was an obstacle he had to take into consideration. They had surprise on their side, but Kathrein had a home-field advantage.

Rush had insisted she leave her phone at the office so Sam could use it as part of the game plan, forwarding any messages from Kathrein to a clean cell phone. The tactic also sheltered Lucy from any unnecessary angst from the old bastard. The pictures of

Jackson had ceased and the messages had gone from aggressive to all-out menacing after the pictures of Lucy and Rush having coffee had been distributed over the internet.

His phone vibrated on the table and Lucy jerked upright. "An update from Sam," he explained as he read the message. "Kathrein checked in again. Sam implied you're making progress."

"Did he back off or send a picture?" She came over to sit across from him at the table.

Rush swallowed a surge of fear as the rest of the exchange came through, including a series of pictures of Gwen. Her clothes were in shambles and she had a nasty black eye on her tear-stained face. He enlarged each picture, searching for a clue in the surroundings to no avail. Thankfully, Sam would break down each shot pixel by pixel.

"Rush." She reached out and rubbed his hand. "You look ready to kill. What happened?"

He deleted the pictures so she wouldn't see them. Brutalizing Gwen made no sense. Had she tried to escape or had one of the guards turned abusive?

Turning his hand, he laced his fingers through hers. "He's the worst kind of bully," he said. "I can't help being furious." During his time in juvie, he'd run up against boys who did terrible things to maintain their place at the top of the heap.

"I should have known the offer was too good to be true."

"Stop." He held tight when she tried to tug her hand free. "You can't take on any blame for Kathrein. He's cornered and has been, one way or another, for seventy years." And he was leading Lucy into the monster's territory. "This is all on him, Lucy."

"He's trying to protect his family," she countered.

"Now you're playing devil's advocate?"

"I've been wondering…"

He waited.

"How far will we go to rescue my family?"

"As far as necessary."

"How does that make us any different from him?"

"Lucy." He set the phone aside and stood up, rounding the table and tugging her with him to relax on the couch. "First, he started it by terrifying you and your family in order to use you. Finishing a fight, sending a Nazi to prison for present and past crimes puts us a world apart from him."

"That's logic and decency, I know." She pulled her knees to her chest and curled herself into a tight ball of misery. "You have connections capable of lethal action?"

"Absolutely." One perk of working with private security programs. "Does that bother you?"

"It should." She bit her lip. "I don't want to stoop to his level," she whispered. "Promise me your connections won't blindly attack the people following his orders."

Leave it to Lucy to ask for something he couldn't give. "We'll have to agree to disagree on that." He gently uncurled her body, and brought her to rest against him. With his legs framing hers, he stroked her silky hair while she stared out the window. "My goal is to get you and your family out of this alive. If—when—this becomes a tactical rescue, it's better for everyone if we handle it swiftly and quietly." As a friend, Lawton would go above and beyond to help, and Rush wouldn't taint that effort by letting them land in political hot water. "The tactical team knows how to be discreet. A pile of bodies doesn't meet that definition."

"Okay."

"I want him to pay for the hell he's caused you, your family and who knows how many others," he continued. "I'll pass on the documentation from Garmeaux to the proper authorities about his real name. Believe me, if I thought we had the time I'd do that first."

"Good." Her cheek rubbed his chest as she nodded.

He wanted to pick her up and tuck her into bed. They had two more hours before landing and she needed the rest. If invited, he'd happily use that time to make her forget everything but the beautiful passion they'd shared.

In the year since she left he'd often tried to pin-point the moment she became the woman he didn't want to live without. Not the first kiss, though it had been electric. Nor was it the first time they'd made love. Both stand-out moments fueled his erotic fantasies, but neither was *the* moment.

He studied her profile as she studied the dark sky beyond the window. Her high cheekbones and stubborn jaw tempted him. He remembered how she melted when he kissed the smooth skin of her throat, now hidden from his view by her hair. Though he longed to kiss her again, he held back.

The moment abruptly popped to the front of his mind. It was the evening they'd invited Sam and Melva to dinner at the boathouse to celebrate an important contract. Everything clicked into place. Lucy completed the family he'd carefully chosen and trusted implicitly. She'd surpassed his calculated list of pros and cons that focused on business and sex.

He'd bought the ring a few days later and come up with the ideal proposal, but he'd put off asking her until it suddenly became too late. The belated self-awareness didn't resolve anything if he didn't understand her side of the story. "Lucy?" He kept stroking her hair, listening to her soft breath.

"Mmm?"

"Why did you leave me?"

"Oh, Rush." She tilted her head back, her brown eyes full of regret. "This should wait."

"Please, just say it."

"I had to go." Her smile was sad as she traced his lips with her fingertips. She lifted her gaze to him again and spoke clearly. "I'd committed the cardinal sin."

He caught her chin, held her gaze. "You cheated?"

Humor lit her eyes and her lips twisted. "Of course not. I fell in love with you."

"You left because you loved me?" Just using the L word backed up the air in his lungs. "You left—"

"The rules were always clear between us. I respect your boundaries." She sat up a little. "I couldn't hold back my feelings anymore and I refused to put that pressure on you."

"What about the new guy in Chicago?"

"There was no new guy. I lied to drive you away." Her cheeks turned pink while she traced the Gray Box logo on his shirt. "If we're being honest, there hasn't been anyone for me since you."

He could hardly process her admission. "You're serious." She nodded. "God, you're clever." He cupped her head and brought her lips to his for a kiss designed to make up for lost time. Her hair sifted over his skin and his body clamored for more thorough action than he could hope for on this couch. Although the bedroom was a few paces away, he held himself in check. *Again*.

Slowly, he steered their deep, passionate kisses to a sweeter place.

"If you're angry, remember you asked," she said.

He caught her as she tried to get up. "I'm not angry." Not even close. He cleared his throat and cuddled her close to his chest. "You should rest while we have the chance." He rubbed her back, threading his fingers through her hair until her muscles relaxed again. Finally, her long, sooty eyelashes brushed her cheeks as sleep claimed her. Rush carefully extricated himself from under her and tucked a blanket over her so she wouldn't wake up chilled.

She'd left because she *loved* him. Did she still? Did he want her, too? Hell, yes.

He pushed a hand through his hair and tried to breathe. Pouring a drink, he indulged in a vision of life surrounded with Lucy's *love*. Days filled with her acceptance, laughter and intelligence had been pure bliss. How much better could it be if he gave her space to express her heart, as well? Unbidden, he saw himself walking to the park near the boathouse with a dark-haired little girl who had Lucy's big brown eyes.

The image didn't put panic in his chest, only a warm, easy joy. He waited for the noisy, wounding echoes from his broken childhood to erupt, and instead he heard Lucy's voice showering him with *I love you*s.

Wow. How had he missed her feelings? How had he ever been so foolish as to let her get away?

They would get through this and then he'd give her everything he should have given her a year ago. They'd have a heartfelt talk about their future, together. Whatever she wanted, whatever she needed, he knew now he could be that man for her.

France, near Strasbourg
Saturday, December 19, 6:30 a.m.

JUST OVER TWO hours later the plane touched down on a private airstrip in northeastern France. Watching Lucy come awake always stirred him. Today was no different. As she stretched her luscious body, his responded instantly. *Later*, he promised himself.

"We're here?"

"Yes. We'll be at the villa I rented within the hour and should have our first views of the winery shortly thereafter."

"Good." She folded the blanket and slipped on her shoes. "How can I help?"

He grinned at her and held out his hand. "Just stick with me." He managed to shut his mouth before he could modify that request to encompass the future. They left the plane and moved quickly to the waiting car. Although he'd given instructions for the gear and luggage, out of habit, he oversaw the transfer of the tech gear before joining Lucy in the back of the sedan.

"Do you have people standing by regional airfields all over the world?" she asked.

"No," he admitted with a brief laugh. "I just know who to call to make it look that way." She pulled back and he missed the closeness all the more after talking and holding her on the plane. "My money never bothered you before." She was one of the few people who'd never been cowed by his net worth or treated him like a walking wallet.

"It doesn't bother me now," she said, wiggling a bit in the seat. "You and Kathrein are so different."

"How so?" he asked, giving in to curiosity.

"I've been around many wealthy people," she began. "Kathrein generally uses his money as a weapon and a shield, leaving his daughters to serve as his public presence and run his charities. Do you think they know who he really is?"

"No. If they knew, they would have circled the wagons by now." He wouldn't let her dodge the question. "Other than being younger and far more handsome, how else am I different?"

She smiled bit and her voice was quiet when she spoke. "You've always splurged the most when you're helping others."

He thought of the extravagant diamond ring he'd bought for her. "You're not a charity case, Lucy."

"Hmm." She slanted a dubious glance at him. "Without your resources and assistance, I would have been forced to cooperate with Kathrein to save Gwen and Jackson."

If he dwelled on the likely outcome of that scenario, he'd break out in a cold sweat. Unable to resist, he pulled her close to his side. She leaned in, resting her hand on his thigh as she'd done countless times before.

"I did consider what a breach would do to your business and reputation."

"But not the damage to our friendship if you'd blown in and out of my life again?"

She smoothed her palm over his knee. "I didn't think we had any friendship left."

That made him inexplicably sad. "Do you want to know how I got through?"

"Got through what?"

"Your move to Chicago," he said with more edge than he'd intended.

She looked up at him. "How?"

"I told myself it was temporary, that you were scared. I convinced myself you needed to test your wings, in business and with men, so you could come back and be sure about us." The car swayed along the winding road and her body leaned into his. "I will always be your friend," he promised, pressing a kiss to the top of her head. He'd be her friend until she was ready to say those words again and trust him with her heart.

She didn't reply and they made the rest of the trip in silence, the ramifications of what they needed to do settling over both of them.

The driver turned off the main road, aiming for a sprawling stone villa at the edge of the valley. "When we're unloaded, I'll set up the drones and we'll confirm whether or not Kathrein is keeping your family at the winery."

She leaned forward to peer at the house as they turned into the drive. Then she shot him a grin over her shoulder. "Some rental." She shook her head. "I'd like to meet your travel agent."

He grinned back at her and had to tease. "If we like the place, I'll buy it."

"No need." She unbuckled her seat belt as the car came to a stop. "The flights would be bad enough, but France has lost the glamorous appeal that originally charmed me."

He pushed open his door and brought her across the seat to exit the car on his side. Pausing, he reveled in the play of early morning light shimmering over the house. "Maybe we shouldn't let one bad apple spoil everything."

She opened her mouth to protest and he silenced

her with a kiss. "I know," he whispered, pulling back. "I know it seems impossible, but we will rescue Gwen and Jackson."

"I believe you." She stared up at the house. "I believe you," she said with more conviction.

He urged her ahead and Lucy pushed open the big front door. He'd specifically requested no staff on site as a way to manage risk and rumors. He and the driver set the luggage just inside the door, then moved the gear Rush had brought along to the garage. With that task complete, Rush tipped him well for his time and silence.

In the garage he and Lucy set up a workshop area with his computers, and the gadgets and gear for the drones and cameras. As each device was unpacked and checked out, he made some final tweaks to the program. After a quick conversation with Sam back in San Francisco, he was good for the test run.

Lucy worked efficiently and quietly. She didn't ask questions or toss around theories. In the uncomfortable silence, faced with the sadness and worry in her typically bright eyes, he hated Kathrein with a barely leashed violence. It was a good thing Lawton's team would keep the creaky old bastard out of Rush's reach.

He didn't care who Kathrein had paid off along the way. He had two days to find a solution that gave Lucy a happy reunion with her family. If the tight time frame meant he had to take a few chances, so be it. He would never give her cause to regret confiding in him or accepting his help.

UNABLE TO HELP Rush further, Lucy went inside to explore the villa. The driver had gone and it was only she and Rush until his friends on the security detail arrived. Only her, really, as Rush worked methodically on the reconnaissance technology. If this sprawling house had the character or history of the place where she and Gwen had stayed on Kathrein's estate, those details were hidden behind luxurious upgrades now. That was fine with Lucy; she didn't want any reminders of her foolishness.

Hauling the luggage up the wide sweeping staircase that dominated the foyer, she halted in the hallway. Did she take both suitcases into one suite or did she keep her distance and maintain the status quo with separate bedrooms? Her lips tingled as she relived the sensual promise in those kisses on the plane.

She couldn't get a read on him to know if they were working their way back together or if Rush was merely being kind and patient until her crisis was resolved. Better to follow his example and keep her mind on the trouble that brought them here. She rolled his suitcase into one room and hers into the room across the hall before she hurried back down the stairs.

In the kitchen, the cold reality of the thumb drive and cloned phone sitting on the counter depressed her. What if they were wrong and Kathrein wasn't holding her family hostage at the defunct winery just beyond the rolling hills to the west?

This was day five of her allotted seven. There wouldn't be enough time to search again, even with Rush's vast resources. She had to keep biting back the plea to let her make contact and arrange an exchange. Overcome, she dropped onto the bench of the banquette in the breakfast nook and let loose a flood of useless tears. Better to get it out of her system now. Her sister and nephew meant nothing to Kathrein. They were pawns he'd crush without a second thought if she didn't deliver. He might kill them anyway.

The glimmer of hope she'd felt when they left San Francisco had faded the closer they came to the confrontation and she realized how little she could help. She couldn't assist or market her way out of this. She had *nothing* to contribute to a rescue plan. After reading the damaging information, she realized no amount of artful dealing would change Kathrein's mind. He would gladly sacrifice her family to save his.

She dried her cheeks with her sleeve and then went in search of a tissue for her nose. Helplessness had never been her strong suit. Weeping and wringing her hands wouldn't make a difference. She needed a diversion.

Her stomach rumbled and she assumed Rush would be hungry, too. He often forgot to eat when he was in problem-solving mode. Several things about him felt different the last few days, yet the basics hadn't changed. Thank heavens he hadn't asked her outright if she still loved him.

With a self-deprecating snort, she gave herself points for being able to help with sustenance. Poking around the gourmet kitchen, she found the basics on the pantry shelves and the refrigerator stocked with everything from wine and milk to thick steaks and vegetables. A fresh pizza had been prepared and wrapped in plastic ready to pop into the oven. A tent card from the property management company topped a fruit basket and had both phone numbers and website links to order groceries. Even a link to a recipe site was listed.

Lucy wondered if anyone from the rental company or the grocery in the nearest town were still in Kathrein's pocket. Maybe not if it had been several years since the family had been here. They would know soon enough.

Choosing convenience, she pulled out the pizza and set the oven to preheat while she searched the cabinets for a pizza stone. Crouched behind a counter, she jumped to her feet when a door opened with a bang and Rush called her name.

"Kitchen," she answered, raising her voice.

He hurried in, breathless, his presence shrinking the massive space. Excitement rolled off him in waves. Even with the big marble island between them, he smelled of sunshine and rich soil and…the masculine scent she'd burrowed into at night when her world had been perfect. Why the hell had she left him?

"Look!" He held up a tablet and waved her over to his side of the marble island. "We're in the right place."

She tripped over her feet at the news and he caught her, steadied her. "You're sure?" The answer was evident in the bright glow of victory in his gorgeous blue eyes. "Oh, thank God. Show me."

He swiped the screen and she watched the replay of a short video.

"Gwen." She blinked back tears of joy and relief as she watched her sister pushing a stroller along a circular patio behind a stone house, smaller than this one. She kept her head down and Lucy's heart ached. But her sister was alive. Thank God. Thank God. A different angle showed Jackson bouncing his arms, oblivious to the danger they were in. "He let them outside?" she asked, startled Kathrein would take the risk.

"They aren't alone." Rush panned back and pointed

out the burly men standing guard at each corner that might offer Gwen an escape. "Unless she bolted into the overgrown vineyard, there's no room to run."

Lucy had to swallow the lump of emotion clogging her throat. "When was this?"

"About an hour ago," Rush replied, beaming. "There's another guard with the car in the front drive. Kathrein must be inside."

"When can we get them out?"

"I've spoken with Lawton and it will require at least one more flyover, but the team will be here in plenty of time. We just have to keep stringing him along."

The relief was a palpable force coursing through her bloodstream. Gwen and Jackson would survive. "Thank you." She gave in and threw her arms around him. "Thank you!" Her lips found his and she gave him a kiss packed with the rising tide of gratitude.

Distantly, she heard the tablet clatter to the marble countertop as Rush's hands clutched her hips. His palms swept up her back, bringing her body flush to his. Her nipples peaked against the hard planes of his chest. Too fast and yet not nearly fast enough. She threaded her fingers through his hair as her tongue swept into his mouth.

His taste electrified her, simultaneously familiar and new. She'd missed this, missed him. "Rush..." Lucy let her head fall back as his lips and tongue and teeth nibbled the sensitive skin up and down her throat. Her hands fisted in the fabric of his shirt, tugging it free of his jeans. Smoothing her palms along the firm, warm skin underneath, she moaned.

He squeezed her backside, flexing his hips to hers. His arousal was obvious and she wanted him inside her now. Sooner, if possible.

She fumbled with his belt and the button of his fly. He boosted her to the countertop and spread her legs to stand between them, his kisses drifting across her cleavage. She drew his face to hers, needing his lips, the subtle comfort he offered hidden deep in the desire surging between them. "I need you."

The dark spark of desire flared in his blue gaze, igniting an answering fire in her belly. His kiss, a blatant mating of mouths, sent her pulse into overdrive. She reached for his shirt, flicking open each button until she could push the panels wide, back and over his shoulders. For a moment, his arms were trapped in the fabric.

She reveled in the view of his magnificent chest and her breath caught as she remembered the fun they'd had with far more effective restraints. Gripping his waistband, she dragged him closer and curled her legs around his hips. "Looks like you're mine now," she teased.

"Always have been," he murmured, his kisses tracing her collarbone.

She didn't have time to dwell on any deeper meanings in the words. The sleeve of his shirt tore a bit as he twisted out of it and tossed it aside. His big hands were heavy, sliding up and down her thighs, making her wish she'd worn a skirt instead of jeans.

"Where's the nearest bed?" he asked, his stubble tickling her sensitive skin.

She tightened her grip with her legs. "Please don't make me wait that long."

"Your wish, my command, sweetheart." His thumbs came close to her center, not quite reaching the place where she needed him most. All these layers between them and she was already slick and aching for him. Only him. There was some wild, needy element inside her that only Rush seemed to unlock.

She fused her mouth to his and slid her hands over his chest, sifting through the dark hair, stroking the hard lines of sculpted muscle and following the trail of hair that arrowed under his waistband. He groaned, flexing his erection into her hand as she stroked him. Silk boxers, she realized, smiling inwardly at the wonderful details about him that remained the same.

He dropped his forehead to her shoulder as she teased him, his breath hot and ragged. Suddenly, he bowed her back over one arm and feasted on her breasts. The shift pulled her hand away from her prize, left her clinging to his broad shoulders for balance as he nipped at the puckered tips of her breasts, soothing each sharp sensation with a slow lap of his velvet tongue.

His free hand cupped her through her jeans, promising more sinful pleasure. She gasped his name, ready to beg for a fast release, so close to a climax just from his deft touches through the fabric.

"Now who's trapped?" He traced the curve of her breast. "I could take you right here."

It sounded like a good start. "Please." No point in playing coy when they both clearly wanted each other. She arched closer to the heat radiating from his spectacular body. She could see the strain of holding back simmering through him. "You can take me anywhere you please."

"Lucy." His nostrils flared when she rocked herself against the hand between her legs. "It's been so long."

"Then stop talking." She kissed him, her tongue dueling with his, seeking all the hot pleasure his kisses promised.

He tugged her off the counter, and with her legs wrapped around his lean hips, he carried her into the sitting room, easing her down to the couch. He dropped his jeans and boxers and, nude, reached for her. Though she tried to help and pleaded with him to hurry, he took his time stripping away her clothes and feasting on every exposed inch of her skin as he revealed it.

He brought her to a shattering climax with his fingers, then his mouth, and still she longed for more. She opened for him, body and soul, and he settled over her. Raising her hips, he entered her in one smooth, hard motion.

Yes, this. The beautiful perfection of being re-united soared through her. Her eyes stung with happy tears and she blinked them away. No one knew her the way Rush knew her.

When he started to move, his hips met hers with hard, greedy thrusts. The pleasure rolled through her, building in exquisite waves of passion from the point where their bodies joined and out across every last nerve ending.

Her muscles squeezing his length, she matched his pace and demanded more from both of them. He reached out and captured the tip of her breast between his fingers and she flew apart, clinging to him as an-other climax swamped her. He reached his peak a moment later, calling her name as his body shuddered over hers. She drifted like a leaf on a gentle river current as her heart rate slowed and Rush's ragged breathing returned to normal.

Shifting so he didn't crush her, he brought her back snug against the warmth and solid security of his chest, his arm a comfortable weight at her waist. As her mind wandered through brambles of true love, contentment and closure, his soft snores became a fa-miliar lullaby behind her.

When she woke a bit later with a start, confused and disoriented, Rush's arm tightened around her reflexively in his sleep and she reached back to smooth a hand over his hip. In the shelter of his body the trouble that had forced her back into his world seemed like a nightmare from someone else's life.

But this wasn't one of those whirlwind getaways Rush had frequently arranged for them. They'd come to France to save her sister and nephew from the crazy old man holding them hostage. Although the sex was unarguably a marvelous distraction, the afterglow had faded, letting her anxiety back in.

Slipping out of his embrace, she found a throw and covered Rush's body, primarily to block the superb temptation. He'd been pushing hard since catching her in his office and she knew he needed some rest, too. Pulling on her jeans and shirt, she gathered up the rest of her clothes. Padding to the kitchen, she put the pizza in the oven and then tiptoed upstairs for a quick shower while it baked.

Her body loose and satiated, she waited for the emotions and regrets to jam things up. Nothing had really changed. She still loved him and though he hadn't pushed her away over the news, he didn't claim to be okay with it. That one-way street hadn't been enough for her before. Could it be enough now, if he could accept her as she accepted him?

She gave herself a blast of cold water before she

turned off the taps. Toweling off, she promised herself she wouldn't run away again. She'd talk to him and sort it all out once they rescued her family.

Chapter Eleven

Though he didn't stir, Rush felt Lucy wake up. It wasn't hard to guess what filled her thoughts as she slipped away from him. While her reasons for jumping him hadn't been ideal, he chose to believe that gratitude sex beat fear-of-death sex. He was more concerned about whether or not gratitude sex could be a foundation for winning her back.

He stayed on the couch, weighing the ramifications until the savory scents of the pizza made his stomach growl. Rolling to his back, he scrubbed at his face. With Lucy, he'd experienced that bone-deep affirmation of his best self. She brought out the best in him. In the boardroom, in his brainstorms, and barring this rather frenzied exception to the rule, she usually brought out his best in the bedroom.

He wondered if it was obvious to her that he'd gone a year without sex. He wouldn't mention it, not while she was rightly focused on her family's safe return. It hadn't been intentional and he wasn't looking for praise. By the time he'd recognized the deeper reasons he wasn't clicking with other women, the freeze had gone on too long. His relationship with Lucy had changed something fundamental inside him. Having allowed her to get so close, nothing superficial held as much appeal.

He was desperate to reclaim that connection, yet he wasn't in the habit of showing any vulnerability. This wasn't a business deal and still he couldn't shake the feeling that telling her would backfire and make him sound as if he'd say anything to keep her around. He'd figure it out and turn this unexpected second chance into something that worked for both of them.

No time like the present, he thought. Sitting up, he grabbed his jeans and dragged them on again, not bothering with the rest of his clothes yet.

Although he had people en route for the rescue, he hadn't made any definitive moves to report Kathrein. He didn't want to cause an international incident while her family was trapped, but he didn't want to let the former Nazi off the hook for the current kidnapping or war crimes. Rush wasn't sure he could count on anyone nearby standing up to Kathrein's bribes. Maybe Lucy had an idea. It was high time the two of them got on the same page about that.

Wearing only jeans he strolled into the kitchen, smiling a little to see she'd picked up his shirt from the floor and left it neatly folded on a counter stool. A bit chilled, he put it on but didn't tuck it in.

"Hungry?" she asked, watching with a shy smile as he covered up.

"For you? Always." He walked up and nuzzled his lips to her neck, wrapping his arms around her waist. He wanted to make it clear that once on the couch wasn't enough.

She turned in the circle of his arms, a lovely blush creeping into her cheeks. "I meant for food. The pizza is nearly done." She moved away to check it.

Caring for others was such a Lucy thing to do. Something he'd taken for granted too often. He used the tablet to check for any new data from the drone. Still flying and recording, so that was good news.

"We should talk," he said. Her shoulders stiffened but, with an effort, he kept the conversation on point. "The rescue operation is a go. The team will go in as soon as they arrive."

The timer went off and a spicy aroma filled the kitchen when she opened the oven door. His mouth watered, for the food and the woman.

"But?" she prompted, setting the pizza stone on the stove top to cool.

He tapped his fingers on the counter. "What do you want to do about Kathrein?"

She pursed her lips, her hands fisting in the pot holders. "What I want to do and what we should do are two different things," she said. When she looked up and her gaze met his, he saw the blast of fury in the brown depths. "I wouldn't lose any sleep if he died," she admitted.

"Luc /." He went to her, covering her restless hands with his . Although he hoped, he couldn't be sure it would l e that simple. "I absolutely understand the sentiment."

He cut the pizza and served up two slices for each of them. When they were seated at the table, a glass of wine and water for each of them, he gathered his thoughts as he dug into the meal.

"I've been thinking a lot about this bully that ran the detention center," he said at last. "Sam and I must have dreamed up a dozen violent ways to take him down."

Her mouth parted on a soft gasp. "You never told me that."

"There were plenty of things I should have told you," he said, his pulse hammering in his ears. And plenty of things he wanted to tell her now, starting and ending with "I love you." He reminded himself there would be time to tell her that, and more, for the rest of his life. He would make sure of it. "You've seen the pictures. Sam and I were skinny nerds. We didn't have the ability to take him down. It was just the two of us against him and the friends who watched his back."

Silently, she watched him over her wineglass.

He didn't like to dwell on those days when he'd been so utterly inadequate to meet the challenges. "Being incarcerated motivated me in several areas," he said.

She smiled, still waiting.

"My point is, we had to make a plan to work together," he continued. "Not just to avoid the physical assault but to carve our way through it. We'd agree how to proceed and then the idiot would divide us. He knew how to push our buttons."

"He was doing the divide and conquer routine?"

"It's effective," he admitted. "We let him get away with it too long and it's a lesson that stuck with me."

She prodded the pizza crust, breaking off a small piece and chewing slowly. "I'm angry and scared and I believe he plans to kill my family." She stopped, rubbing her hands on her jeans. "He has too much to lose. Are you afraid we aren't in agreement about Kathrein?"

"I just want us to go in united. His actions and history prove the ruthless, deadly nature of the man hiding behind the recluse facade."

"Believe me I understand he's dangerous. What are you suggesting?"

"If we arrange a meet and you give him the files you found—"

"You let me find," she interjected.

"Semantics." He grinned at her. "He gets the files and he wins. Most likely that ends with him killing all three of you to be sure those reports never surface. Unless you convince him you arranged for the documents to be released if something happens to any of you."

She shivered. "Option two?"

"Do you have any idea if he tried to breach Gray Box on his own?"

"I don't know who he hired, but he said the man failed. He manipulated me because he thought I could sweet-talk you or something." She shook her head. "He completely underestimated you."

How was it she couldn't see how tightly he was wound around her little finger? He'd do anything for her, including throw over his company. What was money except a tool to rebuild something better?

"Rush?"

He shook off the thought, drained his glass of water and set it back on the table. "Option two is to contact Kathrein and let him know you failed and can't break into the box."

She bit her lip. "How does that help?"

He appreciated her trust. "He would need to regroup or come after me."

"Stop it." She pressed her hands to her eyes. "In that case Gwen and Jackson die and I'd be next on the hit list."

He felt terrible for taking this approach. "Lucy, look at me." He waited until she did. "I am *not* going to let that happen."

She held his gaze. "I know you don't want to let that happen," she replied, softly. "I can see the investment you've made here for me and my family, but we both know Kathrein has all the leverage," she finished, fighting back tears.

"He doesn't, not anymore. I'm pushing your buttons now so we can be stronger, united when we face him," he insisted. "He wants you to feel inferior. He'll play on your fear to get his way. We have to be prepared or those fears will undermine our ability to outsmart him."

She took a deep breath, held it. "You're right." She fanned her face. "Keep going."

Her courage would forever dazzle him. "We have the element of surprise. He thinks we're still in the States, not around the corner. We're a team," he added, emphatically. "Kathrein can't risk bringing his family into this. On top of all of that, we have eyes on *him*."

She eyed the countertop behind him and the tablet monitoring the drone. "How long is your drone able to stay out there?"

"It's programmed to fly a random pattern for several hours before returning."

"What if someone on his team spots it and fol-lows it here?"

"The altitude and random route should keep them from noticing anything out of the ordinary," he as-sured her. "If you'll come with me, I'll show you some other features that might give you a little peace while we wait to make the rescue."

LUCY FORGOT THE dishes and followed Rush to the garage to see the other features he believed leveled the field. Thanks to him, her renewed confidence blotted out the fear that had crept up on her. Some-how she and Rush, along with his team, would pre-vent Kathrein's escape and she was eager to get on with the rescue.

At the workstation Rush cued up the live footage from the drone's camera. "Let's see if we can find a weak spot." He pulled up an extra stool for her.

"I didn't realize we could have been monitoring this in real time," she said, awed by the clarity of the live feed. Instead, they'd had stunning sex and a great meal while her sister and nephew remained prison-ers. Guilt nipped her conscience and she pressed her hands between her knees to keep from chewing on her fingernails.

He leaned over and kissed her temple. "Real time would have simultaneously frustrated you and bored you to tears. The flight path spends significant time well away from the target."

It was little comfort but she realized he was absolutely correct as she watched him work. Various searches and commands appeared on one screen while images flashed by in a rapid slide show on the other. "Give me something to do," she said, restless. "Should I check in with Sam?"

"He'll call us." Rush squinted at something on the monitor. "Use my laptop and bring up the history on this place."

She opened up his personal laptop, momentarily stymied by the password field. "Shall I guess or will you tell me the password?"

"What? Oh." He glanced over and she swore he blushed. "You know it, unless you've forgotten."

She typed in the password she remembered from a year ago, stunned and inexplicably flattered he hadn't changed it. Clicking the folder on the main screen, she saw Sam had added a great deal to the property file over the past fifteen hours. "This winery has always been in the family. Kathrein didn't buy it, he inherited. Or rather, he stole his cousin's inheritance."

"Brace yourself, I might stand up and cheer."

Lucy was distracted by the video segments he was reviewing. "My goodness, that camera is amazing."

"Isn't it?" he agreed absently. "Remind me to give

everyone in R & D a raise when we get back." He zoomed in, changing the color filter on the video.

She didn't have a reply for his assumption that she'd return with him to San Francisco. It wasn't as if she had a better option just now, but she didn't want to give either of them a reason to believe she'd used him.

"I'll be damned."

"What is it?"

"Tunnels." He aimed a finger over a recorded feed that was recycling.

She set the laptop aside and stepped up behind him. "Show me."

He slid his arm around her waist and her heart did a quick, happy pirouette in her chest at the easy intimacy. She rested her hand on his shoulder, unable to fight her affection for him even though she knew she was setting herself up for another long, lonely recovery when they parted ways.

He used the mouse to illustrate what he'd found. "This topographical application is a feature we're developing for a potential client. I think we've nailed it."

"Impressive." He'd all but admitted he was inventing for military applications. That was his way, always looking to help someone. "How do we use it?" Without a more familiar map or reference point, she couldn't make sense of the bright colors.

"In this location, the family must have been part of the French resistance." Rush muttered a curse.

"Ironic a Nazi cousin stole their rightful heritage." He scowled at the monitors, leaning forward and bracing his elbows on the table. "What are the odds Kathrein doesn't know about the tunnels?" he murmured to himself. "This could be a huge advantage for Lawton's team."

She sat down and dug back into the property file on his laptop. "He assumed his cousin's identity," she reminded him. "Wouldn't he have access to everything?"

"Did he bother looking is a better question. He was a young soldier with a superiority complex, alone and on the run. Would he really care about anything other than establishing himself as his cousin?"

"Can we go check the tunnels first?" she asked.

His fingers flew over the keyboard, but she knew he'd heard her. "He doesn't have guards anywhere near the tunnels."

"They might have collapsed or been sealed," she said.

"Collapsed would show on the image. Sealed up at the house is possible."

Her adrenaline spiked at the opportunity to *do* something. "He took his family there for vacations. Any normal child would have found every nook and cranny."

"His children aren't there." Rush stood up, pacing back and forth. "He planned this kidnapping quickly, but he's a stickler for detail. If the tunnels were a concern, he'd have men standing guard."

She laughed, a bitter sound that broke Rush's thoughtful concentration. "Sorry." She clapped a hand over her mouth. "I can't help it. The idea that Kathrein has had possession of a Resistance house all this time and been too self-absorbed to learn the real secrets is bizarre."

Rush gave her a long study. "What are you willing to risk to find out?" He caught both her hands in his. "The way the winery and cellar are situated, I worked up two ideal attack options for Lawton's consideration. We could take a walk and see about giving them a third choice."

A walk through the French countryside at twilight sounded daring. And possibly romantic under different circumstances. "If we're spotted we blow our element of surprise."

"We're two random lovers out for a stroll." He ran his palms up to her shoulders and back down. "No guards around this end of the tunnel." He grinned at her. "And Kathrein has no idea we aren't in San Francisco."

Lovers. The word derailed her thoughts for a moment. If only that could be true again. If only so much more could be true in the future. Unlikely as that outcome was, her mind reached for more practical concerns. "If the tunnels are open, maybe we can get them out tonight."

Hope swelled through her.

"Let's start with a walk and go from there."

She nodded stepping away from him, missing his touch immediately. "Let me change clothes."

"Choose something dark. I'll shower and do the same," he added, falling in behind her.

In less than half an hour they were back in the garage, debating whether or not to go for a drive through the area first when the replacement cell phone rang. The caller ID showed Kathrein's personal number.

"Pick it up," Rush urged. "It will show you're in California. Put it on speaker."

"Got it," she whispered and accepted the call. "Hello?" Her voice fractured as she answered.

"Lucy?"

Lucy's knees turned to jelly at the sound of her sister's voice. "Gwen!" She reached for Rush's hand. "Are you okay?"

"He took Jackson." The rest of her words were lost in a series of sobs.

"What? How'd you get the phone?"

Gwen sniffled. "He gave it to me." Her voice gained some strength. "Told me to call you."

"Tell her!"

Lucy and Rush exchanged a look at the sound of Kathrein barking the order in the background.

"Whatever he wants, Lucy," Gwen gasped. "Do the right thing. Do *not* give it to him. I love you. Jack's waiting for both of us," she finished, shouting the last words amid an audible scuffle.

Lucy jerked at a feminine cry of pain.

Kathrein's rasping voice came on the line. "Do you hear?" Another agonized wail soared through the garage. "Stop flirting about with your lover and bring me what I need. Time is running out for your family, Ms. Gaines."

The call ended and Lucy stared at the device in horror, as if it were a bomb ready to level the villa. Her hands trembled and the shivers moved up her arms until her entire body shook uncontrollably. "He's hurting her," she said in a ragged whisper. "Who knows what he did to the baby."

Rush wrapped his arms around her, bringing her head to his chest and smoothing her hair, stroking a hand up and down her spine, over and over. "We'll get them back, Lucy."

"She's been through so much," Lucy said into the soft cotton of his black sweater. "The baby's arrival… They were so happy. Then Jack died and…and…" She just couldn't finish it. Gwen had been broken and lost and there had been a few weeks when Lucy wasn't sure the baby would be enough of an anchor for her sister's heart. She poured it all out for Rush as he held her. Leaning on his strength now as she'd wanted to do so often then. "Gwen is smart. She might not know why Kathrein started this, but she clearly knows how it is meant to end."

"There's a way to stop him," Rush insisted. "No one is invincible."

"Just like no system is impenetrable?"

He tipped up her chin and she had to look into his eyes. "You got into my system." He feathered a kiss over her forehead.

"Only because I remembered the things you talked about with such passion." She made herself step back, testing her resolve. "I don't want to cave to his demands or damage your Gray Box reputation, but I can't allow my family to die for the preservation of his."

"Let's take that walk," Rush suggested. "The fresh air will clear your head."

She supposed it wasn't too strange that he'd remember that detail about her. His mind was a steel trap of facts and trivia. Bundling into the dark coat and gloves Rush provided, she felt like a spy in cashmere, though the warm garments didn't erase the vicious chill of the circumstances.

Rush sent details of the call to Sam and Lawton. He took her hand and they set off toward the hills in the west, leaving the villa behind them as they followed the road toward the winery.

"What if someone in town saw the drone?"

"Altitude," he replied. His shoulder brushed hers as he shrugged. "Even if it was spotted, we won't be here long enough to get found."

"Not what I'm worried about."

"He can't have spies everywhere, Lucy."

"Okay." She knew paranoia had seized her, but her sister's plea to let them die kept ricocheting through Lucy's head. "He'll kill them whether I cooperate or not."

"We've known that for some time."

She'd known it on some level since this nightmare began. "I didn't know it soon enough to say no to his job offer."

His hand squeezed hers as they walked along. "Why is it you could tell me no easily enough when I wanted to hire you with your sparkling new MBA degree?"

She slid a glance his way, but it was impossible to read his expression in the deepening shadows. "You didn't need me. Me working for you would have only propelled us faster to the inevitable breakup."

"You were that sure we wouldn't make it?"

The sorrow in his voice startled her. "I wanted us to make it." She still regretted that she'd handled it so poorly. "You were a great boyfriend." She squeezed his hand. "When I showed up in Chicago, Gwen called me an idiot for walking out. Well, she used the term 'running away.'"

"Did you ever consider my average daily bank balance as a reason to stay?"

"No." The words stung. One minute he seemed to know her so well and then he'd lump her in with the other women he'd known. "You actually thought I was that shallow?"

"No. But you're the only one I've found who isn't."

"For the record, I recently decided my ideal man has a net worth of only half a million."

"Shh." He tugged her away from the road, down the slope of grass and up another small hill. He stretched out on his stomach and crept up the rise. "That's the Kathrein winery."

She mirrored him, flattening to her belly on the cold ground. "Where is the closest tunnel access?"

He pointed out to the right. "Near the creek. Let's watch for a few minutes and see how far out he sends the patrol."

His deep voice rumbled through the dark, stirring her. He rubbed her arm, then her back, creating all sorts of inappropriate fires within her. She let Rush worry about time, and she used the necessary silence to watch and pray for her family. Other than the guard who strolled back and forth behind the two buildings, the area seemed totally deserted.

"He must have at least one additional man for every guard we see," he whispered. "There's one in front and one floater according to the drone images."

She had to accept his tally as she only saw the one man. "Can Lawton's team handle six men?"

"And more." Rush agreed. "In the pictures, it seems as if it's the same guard all the time beside Kathrein."

"That must be David. I don't recall a time, day or night, when he wasn't close by."

"You did a lot of night work for a ninety-six-year-old man?"

"No." She elbowed him. "There were a few overseas calls those first two weeks. He was adjusting some investments." The guard seemed to turn their way. "Can we go now?" she murmured.

"To the winery tunnels or back to the villa?"

Gwen's screams were fresh in her mind. "The tunnels." She'd do anything to sneak Jackson and Gwen out of Kathrein's clutches tonight.

"Good answer." Rush rooted through his pocket and pulled out a new gadget she didn't recognize. "Let me do one more test, then we'll go."

Rush aimed a gadget at the guard and waited. After another adjustment, he tried again and this time, the guard tapped at his ear, then called for a test of his communications device. "It works," Rush said. "Great range, too."

"Won't that tip them off?"

Rush's teeth gleamed white in the dark when he

smiled. "No way. Technology glitches are a fact of life."

Praying hard, Lucy scooted back down the slope after him and they jogged toward the creek to follow it to the tunnel door.

Please, God, keep them safe.

Chapter Twelve

Rush appreciated Lucy's willingness to check out the tunnels. This could very well be the best way in and out for Lawton's rescue team. Knowing it was smarter to sit back and wait, he told himself the information would empower the team. The problem was after that call from Gwen, Rush knew Lucy's family didn't have much time left.

He checked the map with an app on his phone, confirming his location when they reached the right point on the bank of the creek. He pressed through a stand of scrubby trees and found a low opening. No door, but he checked the area for any alarms or wiring for explosives. Finding none, he continued deeper into what felt like a narrow, natural cave. He turned on a flashlight and, taking Lucy's hand, led them deeper, hoping for the best.

When they encountered the first signs of supports, old timbers in an arch, he breathed a sigh of relief.

"This could be a wild goose chase," he warned. "We can turn back and report it to the team."

Lucy's stared at him with ironclad determination. "We go on."

He knew she was hoping to get Gwen and Jackson out safely tonight. Unfortunately, the odds of that were low. Sneaking in was just the first problem. They had to avoid armed guards and find mother and son, supposedly in separate locations. Although Sam was tracking Rush and Lucy, they didn't carry weapons. Rush forced himself to slow down and take it one step at a time.

Information for Lawton. Rescue if possible. When they were safely away, they could find an official willing to charge Kathrein for his crimes. He had to know someone who knew someone in the State Department who would haul Kathrein in for kidnapping two Americans.

"If we're spotted, promise me you'll run like hell for the villa and call Sam. He will know what to do."

"Sure," she agreed, a little too quickly to be convincing.

He supposed that made them even, though he would have preferred otherwise. Nothing they encountered would force him to leave her behind, either. "No sign anyone's been here in years," Rush pointed out.

"That's good, right?"

"Yes." Every few yards, he paused to check for surveillance gear, relieved they weren't finding any.

"We have to be close," she whispered when he stopped once more.

"Wait here while I look ahead."

"No." She gripped his hand hard. "Forward or back, we stick together."

He nodded, signaling for silence as they inched along the dusty tunnel. Focusing on each footfall, pausing to listen, didn't keep him from replaying her earlier words. What had she meant by "inevitable breakup"?

How had they been completely at odds over where they were headed as a couple? Through hindsight, he could see why she believed he'd resist any emotional declaration. Back then they could talk candidly about anything except her feelings. He hated that he'd let her down and yet his hope for winning her back gave him something to look forward to when they were out of this mess.

The tunnel widened abruptly and the path was partially blocked by barrels and the thick fragrance of rich wine and dry earth. Seeing the winery logo branded on the barrels, he turned off the flashlight. In the absolute darkness, he listened for any sound, hearing only his pounding heart and Lucy's soft breath beside him.

He wanted to send her back and knew she'd never

go. Just as he started to suggest they both turn back and wait for the experts, a baby's cry sliced through the silence.

Lucy jerked forward instinctively and he caught her around the waist. Although he admired her courage in all things, he couldn't let her blow their cover or barge through the door first.

"Careful," he whispered at her ear. He felt her nod once, her cheek brushing his, even as her hands pushed at his hold. "Let me lead."

She dug in her heels, tugging on his arm until he stopped. Pulling his face close to hers she kissed him with an intensity that reached straight into his chest and shook out the cobwebs in his heart. "If you get hurt I will kill you," she murmured against his lips.

He wound his arms around her waist, hugging her so his heart wouldn't drop to the dirt floor and get trampled. "You know how I feel about equality in a deal."

He felt her lips curve into a smile until the baby cried again. They moved stealthily around the barrels and down the cleared space to a door. The old latch creaked as he raised it and the hinges popped and groaned. So much for surprise, he thought, grateful there hadn't been any visible alarm.

They were at the end of a long narrow cellar, under the secondary building. Racks, long empty, stretched along one side, some big enough for barrels, others for bottles. The only light drifted from a bulb at the far end of the cellar, farthest from the tunnel access and closest to the sounds of the distressed infant.

"Where is Gwen?" she asked, mouthing the words.

It would be more efficient to split up and search, but he didn't want to risk it. If they caught her, he knew he'd give up anything for her safety.

Considering Kathrein's impatience to resolve the situation, Rush had to believe he'd set aside one room for his hostages. Easier to control and manage with a mere skeleton crew of his most loyal guards that way.

Keeping Lucy behind him, he moved toward that one lonely bulb. As they approached, he could see three doors set into the walls, two on one side and a third opposite the first. An archway gave way to stairs leading to the upper level. Fully aware that a patrolling guard could come by at any moment, he peered through the small window in the nearest door. The room was dark and he raised his flashlight. But it was empty except for tumbled racks that must have held a prestigious reserve when the winery had been in business.

He moved to the next door with Lucy's hand locked around his. He repeated the process. This time his flashlight found Jackson, wriggling and fussing in a crib that looked as old as Kathrein, only far less sturdy with the spindles and cutouts.

Suddenly Lucy gasped and yanked at Rush's arm,

pulling him back just as a heavy fist swung past his face.

The blow glanced off his shoulder with enough power to turn him sideways. Rush let the spin carry him into the fight, drawing the guard back and away from Jackson's cell. With any luck, Lucy would be able to get the baby out of there.

He traded punches with the bigger man, losing his breath when a ham-sized fist connected with his ribs. Another thing he'd learned in juvie was how to fight dirty. He pulled a Taser from his back pocket and when the guy came barreling at him, he zapped him, sending him to the floor in a jerking, quivery heap.

"Lucy?" He sucked in air as quietly as possible, using the wall for support as he made his way back to Jackson's cell.

"He fooled us." Temper whipped through her voice as she held out a doll.

"What the—" He never finished the question, silenced by a hard strike against the back of his head.

LUCY WATCHED, HORRIFIED as they dragged Rush up the stairs ahead of her. The man holding the gun to her back wasn't necessary, she had no intention of leaving without Rush or her family.

Obviously, Kathrein had known about the tunnels and left them unguarded outside, the ace up his sleeve. She wanted to claw his eyes out for winning this battle, but the war wasn't over yet. Rush was strong and healthy enough to recover from that fight and she was ready to negotiate with the monster if that's what it took to get them all out of this.

On the upper level, the guards pushed open the wide doors of a cavernous room and chained Rush to a thick, support pillar. The guards searched them both for devices and weapons, confiscating everything and powering down the tech gear. Without Sam keeping tabs on them, they'd be alone now. Her impatience had backfired.

She was secured with zip ties to the steel pipes on the end of the old wine bottling line.

"Where is my family?" She made her demand in French, then English. Neither query resulted in a flicker of recognition from the closest guard. "Jean-Pierre!" she snapped, letting him know she recognized *him*. "Tell me where they are."

The guard turned his hard gaze on her. "He keeps them close, treats them as if they are family."

If that was meant to be a comfort, it failed.

"Are they okay?"

With a nearly imperceptible shrug, he moved away, taking up a post near the stairs, his back to the cellar below.

"Rush?"

He groaned an affirmative response and lifted his head as he came around.

She didn't have time to offer him any encouragement or even pretend to come up with an escape plan as another of Kathrein's men walked straight up to Rush and started pummeling his midsection, using him like the heavy bag in a gym.

In shock, Lucy begged him to stop. "Wait, please." She swiveled around. "Jean-Pierre!" she shouted. "Tell Kathrein I have what he wants on a thumb drive."

"No such item was on your person," Jean-Pierre replied.

"I have it, I swear. I came to hand it over."

The guard beating Rush landed another rapid series of jabs and he groaned. She prayed his injuries wouldn't be life threatening.

"You do not have what he wants or you would have come to the door like a civilized person," Jean-Pierre said from his post.

"Don't you dare act as if any of this is civilized," she roared. "I will hand it all over if my family and Rush are released without further harm."

The brute plowed fists into Rush's belly.

"Please, please," she wailed. "You'll get nothing if you kill him."

"I'll get whatever I like, young lady," Kathrein's voice carried through the space, drawing her full attention. "I don't appreciate being roused in the middle of the night," he added, leaning on his guard, David, as he managed the last steps. He flicked out a hand and the big-fisted lout pounded Rush again.

She could practically hear Kathrein's joints grinding as he approached her. He stooped close, his beady eyes cold and mean. "If you have the information, give it to me."

"Allow my family and Rush to leave without further harm and it's yours."

"Don't," Rush said, getting a heavy backhand across his jaw for the effort.

"It was always mine," Kathrein sneered at her. "My secrets should have remained buried. When I verify you are speaking the truth, I will release your sister and nephew." He clapped his arthritic hands and David handed him a tablet. "Release her hands so she can prove she is an honest girl."

Jean-Pierre released her right hand, leaving her left secured to the pipes.

Lucy typed in the access code as Sam had taught her and showed Kathrein the reporter's empty Gray Box. "I downloaded the files to a thumb drive before I deleted them from the cloud, as you instructed."

"Where is this thumb drive?"

"Lucy, don't do it," Rush said. "You know he'll renege."

"Let them go first," she said.

"A compromise." Kathrein signaled David and a large door across the room rolled open. Lucy sagged with relief to see Gwen and Jackson alive. "You honor them with this," Kathrein said almost wistfully. "Family is important."

"We were never a threat to *your* family."

"No, but your man is." Kathrein's black eyes turned mean. On his order, the door closed on Gwen and Jackson.

"No! We had a deal."

"You changed that deal, bringing him here."

"Are you kidding?" Inside, Lucy cringed as she delivered the lie. "I seduced him to get what you wanted. Do the right thing and let them go."

"You've left me only one option for how to proceed."

Despite the shoulders hunched from age and the wispy white hair, Kathrein's mind remained sharp and devious. She knew he had zero incentive to honor his agreement with her. In her impatience, she'd walked Rush into a trap. Panic set her blood pounding through her veins as she sought the words that would save her family and the man she loved. "Release them now or you'll have no options."

"You're hardly in a position to make demands," he snarled.

She smothered a scream, glaring at him and searching for a way to turn the tables. She'd shown enough fear and cowering respect. Rush had prepared her for this. She needed another tactic. "Let us all go or my failsafe will kick in."

Kathrein leveled his full attention on her once more. "Failsafe? You would never be so foolish."

Lucy figured she could milk this approach long enough to buy time for Rush's security team to show up. Sam would have leaped into high gear as soon as their tech had been powered off. "Quit while you're ahead, Kathrein. Your past isn't the only problem now. You've kidnapped four American citizens. You'll have your choice of charges to fight when the press hears about this. What will happen to your grandson's political aspirations then?"

He leaned close to her, his garlic-laced breath moist against her skin. "Word will not get out. None of you will get out. Your failsafe is useless against me."

"We backed up the reporter's research with a Gray Box ghost," Rush mumbled. "I will make sure your secrets go public."

"He's lying," Lucy cried, praying he'd shut up before they hurt him again. "Let them go and I will stop the failsafe."

Kathrein swatted her across the cheek with his cane. The painful thwack of hard wood against her cheekbone startled her into silence.

"Prepare her," Kathrein said. "We will see who is lying."

"Mr. Kathrein, this is your last chance." The cane whipped across her knees this time, bringing tears to her eyes. "Let them go."

Jean-Pierre cut away the zip tie and hauled her to a chair bolted into the floor closer to Rush. Obviously this wasn't the first time they'd used the old winery for an ugly, violent purpose.

Her pleas for logic and common sense went unanswered, ignored by the man she'd misjudged so terribly. As her wrists and legs were secured to the chair, Kathrein spoke in low tones to Rush, who paled under the swelling, cuts and blood marring his handsome face.

"There's no such thing as a ghost box," she said, desperate to find another way.

"What do you need, Kathrein?" Rush asked. His words were slurred by pain and his swollen lip. "What will convince you to let them go?"

"Nothing." He stared up at Rush. "I did not survive this long, build up a family from ashes to have it ruined by rumor."

"What rumor? As a Nazi you committed horrible atrocities," she said.

"War is ugly," he replied, his attention locked onto Rush. "What are they worth to you?"

"Name your price and I'll meet it," Rush said.

"Bah!" Kathrein turned away. "I have enough money for the next three generations to live in luxury."

"Care to share your investment strategy?" Rush quipped.

"What I must have is a sterling reputation." Kathrein poked his cane hard into Rush's gut. "How do I stop your pitiful tricks?" he asked Lucy.

"You let us go," she answered. Where was the rescue team? "It's all automated. If I don't give the code at the right interval, your secrets go to the press."

"Nonsense." Kathrein's mouth thinned. Despite the toll of age, it wasn't difficult to picture him terrorizing prisoners. The man showed no remorse over his past and right now she was sure he intended to relive it with gusto. He popped her with the cane again. "There must be a master switch or all sorts of garbage would litter the news."

"Master code is a myth," Lucy groaned, her gaze on Rush. Behind Kathrein's back he mouthed one word, "Me," and she struggled with the implication. She would not aim the madman at Rush. Where was Lawton with the rescue team?

"Let her go." Rush thrashed against his restraints. "When she and her family are safe, I will give you the code."

"Ah!" Kathrein's mean eyes danced between them. "Now we have progress." The elderly man looked giddy with a burst of anticipation. Behind the cell door, she heard a whimper out of Jackson.

Lucy prayed they hadn't just made a tactical error that would get them all killed.

RUSH SAW THE electric cattle prod in David's hand and knew immediately what they intended. They would shock him and make her watch. Classic divide and conquer approach, hoping to make her talk by hurting him. He'd been trying to get Lucy to aim Kathrein at him, but she wouldn't cooperate.

Didn't the old geezer understand Rush, not Lucy, had control of the system he sought to infiltrate? Either the bastard didn't comprehend how the cloud worked or he didn't care.

"Close your eyes, Lucy." Rush hated what she was about to see and he hoped like hell the team would get here before Kathrein's torture fried his brain beyond usefulness. At least if Rush died Sam would be able to carry on, and since he'd updated his will last night with a call to his attorney, Sam and Lucy as partners would keep Gray Box going strong. He took a breath, willing his body to relax as that cattle prod got closer.

But the beady-eyed bastard surprised him, signaling his man toward Lucy. "No!" Rush strained against the bindings. "No! She doesn't know anything."

"She knows more than you think. She is too quick for her own good. Isn't that right, Ms. Gaines?"

"Let us go now and we won't press charges," she said, unaware of the device behind her.

Kathrein cackled. "You do not dictate terms to me!"

Rush fought the chains, instinctively trying to spare her. "Stop. She can't help you."

Kathrein ignored him. "Garmeaux," he shouted. "Who did you talk to about him?"

"No one," she said.

"You're lying. My daughter took a call late yesterday about him."

The guard sent a jolt of electricity through Lucy's body. Her head fell back and her limbs jerked in a macabre dance.

Rush roared, helpless to protect her. Damn it, this was his fault. He'd set Sam loose with the Kathrein family tree and told him to skip the subtlety.

"Stop!" he shouted again.

Kathrein turned, his black eyes gleaming with obvious delight over Lucy's pain. "She betrayed me."

"You've got no reason to cry foul." Rush mustered as much disdain as possible now that he had the old man's attention. "You used her."

"And I will continue."

Rush discarded the idea of playing to the man as a father. Any capacity for sympathy was erased by the sick joy he gained from hurting others. "I can help you. I am the only person in this room who can make your troubles disappear."

Kathrein ignored him. "Lucy, give me the master code."

"I forgot it."

She got zapped again and Rush swore. "Tell him!"

"I used his old password. Erased it afterward."

"Give it to me," Kathrein demanded.

"No."

They pumped more juice into her and Rush forced himself to keep his eyes open, a source of encouragement and strength if she would only look at him.

"Tell him, Lucy," Rush pleaded. Why was Lucy resisting? She had to know Sam would be on the other side of the connection, scrambling to protect the information.

But Kathrein didn't ask again. This time he asked her how the ghost box worked. When she didn't know, the cattle prod zapped her again.

Where the hell was Lawton? Lucy couldn't take much more of this and Rush would never be able to live if Kathrein killed her.

When the room quieted, Rush blurted out the master code.

"No," Lucy protested. "Don't give in."

Kathrein turned and stared at him. "Again!"

Rush repeated it, symbol by symbol while another man typed it into the waiting laptop.

"Well?" Kathrein asked his man. "Does it work?"

Rush caught the wary expressions on the faces of the guards Kathrein employed. Rush knew then that if his team didn't arrive, they would all be dead. Kathrein wasn't after access or secrets anymore. He'd gone off the rails, sliding into a gruesome past he'd enjoyed too much.

"Take what you want," Rush said. "Have a damn field day." Every minute Kathrein was distracted with him or the computer was a minute Lucy could use to recover and another minute for the rescue team to leap into action.

"I feel as if you need some compensation for this generosity," Kathrein said.

"All I want is for you to let them go."

"No." Kathrein cackled, the sound rising into the rafters. "I am not done with any of you."

Lucy wanted to believe she was trapped in a terrible nightmare. Her blood felt as if it had been replaced with fizzy candy. Breathing made her lungs prickle and every nerve ending sizzled independently of the others. She'd give just about anything for that to never happen again.

In a blissful lull, her ears stopped ringing and she heard Rush spell out a code. Kathrein's giddy reply a moment later told her he'd unlocked something special.

Except Rush couldn't have done the unthinkable. There was no scenario where Rush relinquished control of his proprietary system to a madman. But... had he? Why? Had he really opened up all of Gray Box for Kathrein?

Based on the gleeful expression on Kathrein's face, he'd hit the motherlode of information.

Tears slid down her cheeks. Rush was ruined. No amount of money or careful media spin would set this right. "Rush," she whispered, trying to decide which of the three visions of him wavering in front of her eyes was the real one. "No, please, not this." He'd worked every day since his release from juvie to reach financial and creative independence. It had been his sole mission, to make a name for himself and use his skills in a way that helped people and gained respect from the world.

Now, the one time he put something ahead of his business, it would cost him everything. It was too much. "I'm sorry," she said, squeezing the words through her dry throat. Her gaze sought his, held it. "Why?"

His lips moved and she knew she must be hallucinating. The Rush she loved didn't use the L word. Another jolt from the cattle prod seared through her and wiped the thought from her mind as she slid into a blissful blank space.

RUSH WATCHED LUCY pass out and howled, fighting the cuffs that kept his arms over his head. "I will kill you!" he shouted at Kathrein.

The guard brought that damned cattle prod closer, aiming it at him. Finally. Rush tossed out all sorts of threats and dire promises, desperate to divert the focus from Lucy. Shouting and flailing, he didn't hear the first explosion. When the floor trembled and dust rained from the ceiling, hope coursed through him. Lawton and the rescue team were here, at last.

Kathrein's men sprang into action, protecting their boss, but they were no match for the tactical expertise of the rescue squad. Only six men, they seemed to be everywhere, surging up the steps and closing in from all sides.

The battle was brief, typical of a Lawton strike. When the sound of bullets ceased, Kathrein and the surviving guards were secured. Released from his restraints, Rush went straight to Lucy, who remained unconscious. Although his arms felt as if he'd been stretched on a rack and his shoulders screamed, he lifted her against his chest. He carried her outside, where floodlights cast a pale glow over the scene.

"Come on, Lucy." He pleaded with her, momentarily relieved when her lashes fluttered as she came to. Without a word, she slipped away again.

Lawton called for a medic while Rush tried to rouse her again.

"Sister and baby are already out," Lawton stated. "We didn't want them anywhere near a firefight. That was the delay. Are you all right?"

Rush nodded, his only concern was Lucy.

"Any chance of broken bones?"

"Maybe cracked ribs." Nothing to do for that but rest. Rush jerked his chin toward the battery and cables. "I don't think anything's broken for her. She took too many hits from the cattle prod and he nailed her a few times with that damned cane."

Several minutes later, the medic declared her bones intact and waved smelling salts under her nose, getting increasingly alert reactions. She came around, mumbling Rush's name.

"I'm here, sweetheart." He gripped her hand, brought it to his lips.

"You're okay." Her mouth curved into a weak smile. "Thank God."

"My sentiments exactly." He forced his way between her and the medic. "How do you feel?"

"Like I danced in a lightning storm. Where are Gwen and Jackson?" she asked, trying to sit up.

"They're already en route to the airfield," he explained. "You'll see them soon."

"Good." She sagged back against him. "I'm sorry you had to give up everything to get us out of there."

"The company, the money, the reputation," he promised, "none of it matters if I lost you."

The surprise in her eyes at those words shamed him. He never should've left room for her to doubt how much she meant to him. When she was feeling better he'd tell her the whole story about creating not just a failsafe or ghost box, but a ghost company to trap Kathrein. Right now, she needed time to recover.

"What about Kathrein?"

"Sam's been working on that. He has a friend in the State Department I didn't even know about."

Lucy sat up a bit more. "Thank you for saving my family." She wrapped her arms around him, burying her face in his shirt. "For saving us."

He felt the tears through the fabric and held her close, letting her get it all out.

Leaving Lawton at the winery to coordinate the cleanup with Sam's friend, Rush went straight to the airfield so Lucy could be reunited with her sister and nephew. Once they were all on the plane, he gave the order to get the hell out of France. He couldn't wait one more hour to take her home and keep her safe with him behind American borders and his wall of lawyers.

Chapter Thirteen

Christmas morning dawned clear and bright, and Rush had the best gift curled beside him in the king-size bed, her hand resting over his heart. Most of their bruises were healed and he traced her fingers, wondering if she had any idea how precious she was. To her family, to him, to the world at large.

Her courage and bravery astounded him whether they were in the French countryside or in a development meeting. "I love you, Lucy Gaines," he murmured into her hair.

She didn't so much as twitch. Probably better that he had another practice run at that powerful statement. He'd be more convincing if he was used to hearing himself say the words.

He woke her with gentle kisses, having his way with her in the shower before they went downstairs to exchange presents and mimosas with her sister and nephew. It wasn't the most extravagant Christmas on record, that could wait, but it was definitely the sweetest and most significant of his life. It sure beat skiing at a mountain resort with only Sam and a few women they wouldn't remember by St. Patrick's Day.

The three adults traded off between dinner prep and caring for Jackson until at last they sat down to a feast of ham and all the trimmings. Happy as he was to be here with Lucy and her family, Rush wasn't entirely content. He served himself another piece of cherry pie, to the ribbing of both women, and tried to firm up what he needed to say to Lucy and how he was going to say it.

Gwen cleaned up Jackson's hands and face, and carried him to the rocking chair, shooting a look at Rush behind her sister's back.

It is time, that look said.

He knew it. Past time, really. The small velvet box would burn a hole in his pocket at this rate. He'd thought of taking her to dinner or out on the boat with a sunset glowing on the bay. He was sure she needed more space to forget their ordeal. He should—

His thoughts evaporated as she slipped her arm around his waist. "Thank you for a lovely and very merry Christmas, Rush," she said. "This is exactly what we needed."

"Exactly?"

"You've been so gracious to welcome us to the boathouse. This quiet and peace has helped Gwen immensely."

"What about you?"

"I'm happy to be here with you." She smiled up at him, her brown eyes reflecting all the words he couldn't seem to get out of either of them. She'd loved him once and never said it. In the past few days he wondered if her feelings were still as strong and he had a fresh appreciation for how hard it was to keep love trapped inside a heart—even a damaged one— the words unspoken.

"The boathouse has always felt like home when you're here." He led her out to the balcony and let the breeze tease her hair as she leaned into the rail. Impatient, Rush pulled her around to face him, gliding his hands up and down her arms, his eyes locked with hers. "I love you, Lucy Gaines."

There. It was out. What would she do with the news?

"I know. It shows in your every action, big or small." She pressed up on her toes and kissed him and then looped her arms around his waist. "Even when you didn't want to see it, when I didn't trust how you defined it, love was there."

Enchanting as he found her analysis and kisses, he thought he might lose it if she didn't say the words. If he'd missed his chance with her...

"I love you, too, Rush Grayson. I always have."

His heart kicked back into a normal rhythm, flooding him with energy and hope. "We should give your sister the condo on Fremont Street," he blurted out.

She stepped away, frowning a little before she turned to stare out at the choppy water of the bay. "You moved out of here when I left, didn't you?"

"Yes. It hurt to be here alone."

Her shoulders rose and fell. "But it won't hurt you to be here alone now?"

Was he moving too fast for her to trust the words? He couldn't dwell on possible failure and he shook off the doubts. He had to follow through. "Lucy." He dropped to one knee behind her. "I don't intend to be here or anywhere else without you."

She turned and the frown on her face lifted. Her big brown eyes swept over him and then locked on the glittering diamond ring framed in the black velvet box he held open. "Lucy Gaines, will you allow me the honor of being your husband?"

"Rush." She covered her mouth with both hands, her eyes sparkling with happy tears. "When? How?" She fanned her face and then her gaze slammed back to him. "We've been glued at the hip since…since we've been back. When did you have time to buy a ring?"

"Last year," he admitted, wishing like hell she'd give him an answer to the biggest proposal of his life.

"It's been waiting for you—*I've* been waiting for you every day since."

Her hands dropped to her sides. "You're serious."

"Lucy," he said, battling the rising exasperation. "Can you give me an answer?"

She grinned, crossing her arms. "What if I want to negotiate the terms?"

No woman was as perfect for him as this one. "Come down here and give it a try."

She sank to her knees and he immediately worried about the lingering aches from their trouble in France. "Yes, Rush, I'll marry you." She cupped his jaw with her hands. "I only have one condition."

He pulled the ring out of the box and slipped it over the tip of her finger. "Granted."

She stopped his progress. "You haven't heard it yet," she said on a bubble of laughter.

"Don't need to. You've given me everything, Lucy. Acceptance, support, affection and your heart full of belief and understanding. There's nothing you can ask of me that I wouldn't gladly give you."

"You haven't heard it." She pursed her lips. "Maybe I should have my people call your people."

"You are the only people who matters to me, sweetheart. Don't you see that yet?"

"I do, Rush." She let him push the ring all the way into place. "I only wanted to stipulate a weekly date night, no electronics allowed."

"Done." He stood up and pulled her close, kissing her with everything he'd kept bottled up for too long. His heart soared as she matched his affection and passion. "Can we start tonight?"

"Of course." She tipped back her head and laughed as he spun her in a circle. "I'm all yours, for always."

Just inside the door Gwen and Jackson cheered. Following Lucy inside, as his fiancée and his future sister-in-law admired the engagement ring, Rush thought the gift of a loving and exuberant family was the best holiday miracle a man could ask for.

This was the most wonderful Christmas of his life.

* * * * *

INTRIGUE

Available December 20, 2016

#1683 RIDING SHOTGUN
The Kavanaughs • by Joanna Wayne
Pierce Lawrence returns to the Double K ranch a war hero after two tours as a SEAL ready to bond with his five-year-old daughter. Grace Cotton has been on the run from her ex in witness protection, but maybe Pierce and his daughter are the homecoming she's been waiting for.

#1684 ONE TOUGH TEXAN
Cattlemen Crime Club • by Barb Han
Alice Green, a young cop, goes rogue to save a young girl after she believes her actions led to the girl's abduction. Joshua O'Brien knows a thing or two about putting everything on the line. But can Alice open up enough to let the handsome rancher aid in her mission?

#1685 TURQUOISE GUARDIAN
Apache Protectors: Tribal Thunder • by Jenna Kernan
Apache guardian Carter Bear Den rescues his former fiancée, Amber Kitcheyan, from a mass shooting at the hands of an eco-extremist. But Amber is the only living witness—and what she knows might get them both killed.

#1686 BATTLE TESTED
Omega Sector: Critical Response • by Janie Crouch
Rosalyn Mellinger never meant to dupe Steve Drackett, head of the Critical Response Division of Omega Sector—she fled after their weekend of passion to protect him from her ruthless stalker, The Watcher. But now Steve is the only one who can protect her...and their unborn child.

#1687 STONE COLD TEXAS RANGER
by Nicole Helm
Vaughn Cooper is a by-the-book Texas Ranger. Natalie Torres is a hypnotist brought in to crack the witness in an ongoing investigation. It's distrust at first sight, but only together can they withstand the coming danger.

#1688 SAN ANTONIO SECRET
by Robin Perini
When Sierra Bradford's best friend and goddaughter are abducted, she vows to find them at any cost. Even if that means teaming up with former Green Beret Rafe Vargas, who's come to her aid...and not for the first time.

HICNM1216

SPECIAL EXCERPT FROM

*A popular girl goes missing, and everyone
close to her has something to hide.*

*Go inside the mind of a criminal in the fourth book in
the riveting* **THE PROFILER** *series:
STALKED by Elizabeth Heiter.*

"Where are you, Haley?" Linda whispered into the
stillness of her daughter's room.

Today marked exactly a month since her daughter
had gone missing. Since Haley's boyfriend, Jordan, had
dropped her off at school for cheerleading practice. Since
her best friend Marissa had waved to her from the field
on that unusually warm day, watched her walk into the
school, presumably to change before joining Marissa at
practice.

She'd never walked out again.

How did a teenage girl go missing from *inside* her
high school? No one could answer that for Linda. As time
went by, they seemed to have fewer answers and more
questions.

But Linda *knew*—with some deep part of her she
could only explain as mother's intuition—that Haley was
out there somewhere. Not buried in an unmarked grave,
as she'd overheard two cops speculating when day after
day passed with no more clues. Haley was still alive, and
just waiting for someone to bring her home.

Linda clutched Haley's bright pink sweatshirt tighter. She fell against the bed, trying to hold her sobs in, and the mattress slid away from her, away from the box spring.

Linda froze as the edge of a tiny black notebook caught her attention.

The book was jammed between the box spring and the bed frame. The police must have missed it, because she'd seen them peer underneath Haley's mattress when they'd looked through the room, assessing her daughter's things so matter-of-factly.

Linda's pulse skyrocketed as she yanked it out. She didn't recognize the notebook, but when she opened the cover, there was no mistaking her daughter's girlie handwriting. And the words...

She dropped the notebook, practically flung it away from her in her desire to get rid of it, to unsee it. She didn't realize she'd started screaming until her husband ran into the room and wrapped his arms around her.

"What? What is it?" he kept asking, but all she could do was sob and point a shaking hand at the notebook, lying open to the first page, and Haley's distinctive scrawl:

If you're reading this, I'm already dead.

Follow FBI profiler Evelyn Baine as she tries to uncover which of Haley's secrets might have led to her disappearance.

STALKED
by Elizabeth Heiter
Available December 27, 2016,
from MIRA Books.

$1.00 OFF

ELIZABETH HEITER

Secrets can be deadly...

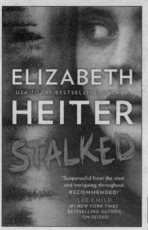

STALKED

USA TODAY BESTSELLING AUTHOR

HEITER

"Suspenseful from the start and intriguing throughout. RECOMMENDED!"
— LEE CHILD, #1 NEW YORK TIMES BESTSELLING AUTHOR ON SEIZED

$7.99 U.S./$9.99 CAN.

MIRA®

Available December 27, 2016

Order your copy today!

$1.00 OFF

the purchase price of STALKED by Elizabeth Heiter.

Offer valid from December 17, 2016, to June 17, 2017.
Redeemable at participating retail outlets, in-store only. Not redeemable at Barnes & Noble. Limit one coupon per purchase. Valid in the U.S.A. and Canada only.

52614428

5 65373 00076 2   (8100)0 12233

THE WORLD IS BETTER WITH

Romance

Harlequin has everything from contemporary, passionate and heartwarming to suspenseful and inspirational stories.

Whatever your mood, we have a romance just for you!

Connect with us to find your next great read, special offers and more.

SERIESHALOAD2015